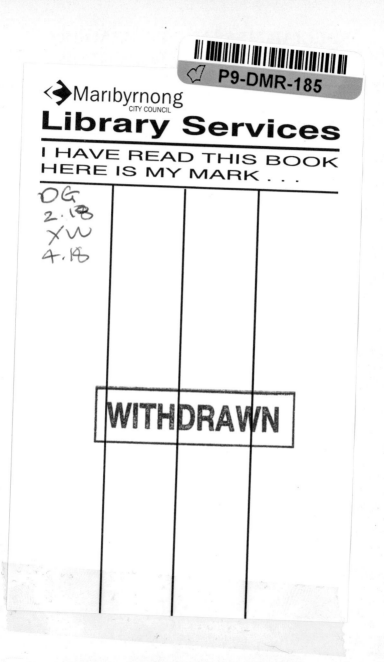

FIT FOR LOVE

Stacey and her stepbrother, Ben, are shocked when Ben's father, Max, announces he is to retire and hand over the reins of his business to Rafe Stocker — a relative stranger to the two siblings. Rafe appoints Stacey as his second-in-command, an offer she feels an obligation to accept, if only to prove that there is room for women in business — something Max has never believed in. But how does Max know the mysterious Rafe, and why did he choose him to run the business? Stacey is determined to find out . . .

MARGARET MOUNSDON

FIT FOR LOVE

Complete and Unabridged

LINFORD
Leicester

First published in Great Britain

First Linford Edition
published 2014

A catalogue record for this book is available
from the British Library.

ISBN 978–1–4448–2045–4

Published by
F. A. Thorpe (Publishing)
Anstey, Leicestershire

Set by Words & Graphics Ltd.
Anstey, Leicestershire
Printed and bound in Great Britain by
T. J. International Ltd., Padstow, Cornwall

This book is printed on acid-free paper

1

Stacey awoke with a jolt. Blinding sunshine poured through the window, creating dazzling psychedelic patterns on a cherry red carpet that jarred the back of her eyes. Surely her bedroom carpet was blue? She felt around behind her head for her pillow. It wasn't there. Neither was her bed.

Careful to make no sudden movement, Stacey tried to get her thoughts in order. There had been a party. There had been no offer of a lift home afterwards. She had decided to sleep over on Emily's sofa. She now remembered why she was curled up underneath a scratchy blanket. It also explained why she had a crick in her neck, cramped legs and a mouth as dry as the Sahara desert.

Stacey groaned again and staggered to her feet. What she needed was a shower, then a coffee in that order.

'I'm off now.' Emily poked her head round the bathroom door.

'Aren't you having any breakfast?'

'It's half past eleven and some of us have to go to work,' Emily trilled back at Stacey.

'It can't be that late,' Stacey mumbled through a mouthful of toothpaste.

'Yes it is,' Emily insisted with a bright smile. 'Can't stop.'

Wrapped in a fluffy towel with another turbaned around her wet hair, Stacey padded back into the living room and, picking up her watch, blinked at the dial. The DJ's voice floated through from the radio in the kitchen.

'For all you sleepy heads out there, hope you didn't forget to put your clocks forward an hour last night. Summertime starts today. March twenty-ninth, and in my book it's the first day of spring. If it's your birthday, many happy returns.'

With a yelp of horror, Stacey sprinted

2

back into the lounge and snatched up her mobile. She punched in Ben's number. 'Come on, lazybones,' she urged through gritted teeth, 'answer the call.'

There was no reply. Leaping into her discarded party dress, Stacey raced back into the kitchen to check the emergency numbers on Emily's corkboard. She ran her finger down it looking for a mini cab.

'Looks like you're another who forgot about the hour going forward,' was the driver's cheerful greeting as Stacey fell into the back seat.

'Stopes Cottage, please,' she gasped, 'and hurry.'

'Normanswood? I'm on my way.'

She was still trying Ben's number as they drew up at the end of Lavender Lane. Thrusting a note into the driver's hand, she jumped out of the cab and ran up the incline as fast as her killer heels would allow.

'Ben.' She rattled the knocker before searching frantically in her clutch bag for a key. A black ball of fur shot past her as she unlocked the door, followed by two rescue grey hounds. Sensing their urgency, she didn't bother calling after them. Ducking her head, she galloped up the stairs and fell into a room at the end of the corridor.

'Wake up,' she bellowed at the lump under the bedcovers. 'It's nearly lunch time.'

'Geroff,' the lump groaned as Stacey whacked at it with a rolled up newspaper.

'It's Sunday.'

'Don't care.' Ben grabbed at the duvet as Stacey began to tug it off him.

'What happened to your alarm?'

'Didn't set it.'

As Ben's hold of the duvet slipped, Stacey seized her moment and dragged it away from the bed. 'If you're not out of bed in two minutes, I'm going for a bowl of water,' she threatened.

'I'll shave myself when I'm ready,' Ben protested.

'I intend throwing it over you.'

'Why?'

'It's Max's birthday lunch.'

'Chill, we've stacks of time.'

'No we haven't. Now move it.'

Scratching at his hair and still grumbling about inconsiderate step-sisters, Ben heaved himself into a semi-recumbent position. 'What happened to the time?' He frowned at his wristwatch.

'We lost an hour last night.'

Stacey began rooting through her wardrobe for something suitable to wear. There wasn't time to blow dry her hair. She would have to tie it back in a bow and hope it didn't frizz up too much. Grabbing at an apple-green button-through dress and a pair of sandals, she thrust them on, then ran back into the corridor. Ben ambled past her in his shorts.

'Hurry up,' she pleaded.

'Coffee,' Ben mumbled.

'I'll see to that. Get in the shower, now.' She shoved him towards the bathroom. It was always the same with

Ben. Not bothering with the percolator, she spooned coffee granules into a mug and flicked the switch on the jug kettle.

'This stuff tastes horrible.' Ben grimaced as he swallowed a mouthful of instant coffee.

'Have you got a clean shirt?' Stacey demanded.

'Not sure.' Ben thrust two slices of bread into the toaster.

'There isn't time for breakfast.'

'Yes there is,' he insisted. 'Dad won't mind if we're a little late.'

'We're more than a little late.' Stacey lugged the ironing board out of the cupboard and began to search frantically through the laundry basket. 'Will this one do you?' She held up a badly crumpled peacock-blue shirt.

'Whatever.' Ben began buttering his toast.

The iron hissed as Stacey slammed it down on the cotton fabric of Ben's shirt. 'Where's the present?' she demanded.

Ben widened his blue eyes. 'What present?'

'The cashmere jumper and golfing trousers we bought for Max last week.'

'No idea.' Ben started on his second slice of toast.

'Ben,' Stacey implored him. 'It's your father's sixty-fifth birthday lunch. We are the guests of honour.'

'I can't understand what all the fuss is about. Dad's never gone in much for birthday parties in the past.'

'Well he has this year, and we owe it to him to be there on time.'

'Don't think we will be.' Ben grinned at her. Stacey steeled herself not to smile back. That was the trouble with Ben. He had charm by the bucket-load and he knew how to use it.

'Right.' He stood up. 'I'm ready. Where's my shirt?' He frowned at Stacey. 'What's wrong with your hair?' he asked.

'Never mind my hair.' She thrust the freshly ironed shirt into his hand. 'Get dressed and don't forget to wear a tie. I'm going in search of Max's present and some wrapping paper.'

'I wonder what this birthday lunch is really about,' Ben mused as he drove along. 'Dad never does anything without a reason.'

Stacey bit her lip. Ben did have a point. As much as she loved her stepfather, she wasn't blind to his faults. After his first wife, Ben's mother, died, he married Stacey's widowed mother and together the four of them had created a loving, if sometimes volatile, family unit; then when Stacey was sixteen, her mother died. Max had always treated her like his own daughter and, although she suspected Ben sometimes resented his father's generosity towards his stepdaughter, they continued to rub along.

Ben's passion in life was art. Stacey admired the way he stood up to his father, refusing to be coerced into working for him. Max was old-fashioned enough to believe that the job of running Wade Manor, the family health club, should only go to a man, and the idea of offering a position to

Stacey would never have entered his head. Not that she was sure she wanted to work for Max either. He had been known to move sensitive employees to tears on more than one occasion.

After she left school, Stacey opted to be a freelance customer relations officer. She enjoyed the variety of not having a regular schedule, and the personal allowance she received from Max meant a week without work wasn't a pressing issue.

Stacey realised, to her horror, that they were over an hour late as they drew up outside the country club.

'Come on then,' Ben said, 'let's go and wish Dad many happy returns.'

The headwaiter showed them to a corner table, where they found Max and one other guest waiting for them.

'Happy birthday, Dad.' Ben shook hands with his father.

'I'm sorry we're late,' Stacey chimed in, handing over the present and kissing Max's cheek.

Her stepfather brushed aside her apology. 'Let me introduce you to Rafe Stocker.'

Stacey frowned. Although she didn't recognise the man standing before her, she couldn't help thinking she had heard his name somewhere before.

'Rafe has come over from Australia. And,' Max added in a tone of voice that suggested he was not best pleased, 'he managed to be here on time.'

'Stacey forgot to put her watch forward last night,' Ben volunteered as an explanation for their late arrival.

Stacey's hissed intake of breath caused Rafe to raise an eyebrow as he shook her hand. 'I'm pleased to meet you,' he said in an accent that betrayed his antipodean origins. 'Your father's description of his daughter didn't do you justice.'

'Stepfather,' Ben put in before Stacey could say anything. 'Stacey is Dad's stepdaughter.'

'Of course,' Rafe agreed with a small inclination of his head.

Stacey tucked a recalcitrant curl of hair behind her ear. It was already beginning to escape the confines of the inadequate ribbon she had hastily tied round it. In the same moment she became aware that the top button was missing off her dress. Even if she had noticed it earlier, there wouldn't have been time to sew on another before they left Stopes Cottage. As if sensing her discomfort, the corner of Rafe's mouth quirked into a smile.

'Only the four of us?' Ben queried as he sat down.

Rafe drew out the chair next to him and made a gesture towards Stacey. 'Perhaps you'd like to sit beside me?'

She accepted his invitation with hastily mumbled thanks, hoping her dress wouldn't gape too much throughout what might be a difficult lunch party.

'Although today is my birthday and this is supposed to be a celebratory meal,' Max began, waving away a hovering waiter, 'there are one or two bits of business I need to get through first.'

Stacey stopped crumbling the bread roll that had been placed on a plate beside her. Ben threw her his 'I told you so' look. 'Can't it wait until a more appropriate time?' he asked his father, casting another cursory glance at Rafe.

'No it can't,' Max snapped back at him.

'I just thought with Mr Stocker not being family . . . ' Ben shrugged, not finishing his sentence.

'Mr Stocker is here as my guest.' The tone of Max's voice brooked no disagreement.

'I hope what you have to say is nothing serious.' Stacey smiled at Max in an attempt to lighten the atmosphere.

'It depends what you mean by serious.' Max paused. 'For reasons of health my doctors have advised me to ease up.'

'You're not ill?' The question caught in Stacey's throat. There were dark circles under Max's eyes, but her stepfather had always worked long hours. He thrived on it, even though his workload would have daunted many a younger man. In Max's opinion, a weekend not spent networking was a weekend wasted.

His eyes softened as he looked in her direction. 'No,' he said gently, 'I am absolutely fine. But at the age of sixty-five, I have decided the time has come to retire.'

'What?' Ben's raised voice drew enquiring glances from the other diners.

'I am handing over the reins.'

'You're not serious?' Ben still looked as though he didn't believe his father.

'It will of course mean a significant change of lifestyle for you both.'

Stacey's heart was thumping so hard it hurt her ribcage. 'You're not selling the cottage?' The shocked question tumbled from her lips.

'Nothing so drastic,' Max assured her.

'That's a relief,' Ben said.

'I don't think I could bear to live anywhere else,' Stacey agreed with him.

13

'Whilst overall control of Wade Manor remains with me, I am appointing a chief executive officer to run things.'

Stacey sensed what was coming next.

Max turned to his son. 'As you have on more than one occasion made your feelings about working for me abundantly clear, I have no other choice. It's time for a younger man to take over the reins. Someone with new ideas and modern business practices.'

'Are you sure you're making the right decision?' Stacey asked.

'If I don't, I will regrettably be forced to close the club down.' Max cast Stacey a sympathetic look. 'There's something else I have to tell you.'

'Not more shocks.' Ben glared at Rafe as if the situation were his fault.

'I find myself in the embarrassing situation of no longer being able to fund your personal allowance, Stacey.'

'Why didn't you say something earlier?' Stacey demanded, annoyed that Max must have known that things were bad for weeks.

'You know my views on involving women in business,' he replied.

'You didn't mention it to me either.' Ben sounded like a petulant child.

Max picked up a glass of water off the table and sipped it.

'Ben's right. Perhaps we could talk about it later?' Stacey suggested as Max swallowed a small pill.

'I'm afraid not. I don't have much time.'

'Are you keeping something else back from us?' Stacey demanded.

'Only the fact that I have booked myself on a Mediterranean cruise and I leave early next week.'

Stacey opened her mouth but Rafe put out a hand and gripped hers, frowning at her to keep silent.

'From today,' Max spoke carefully, 'Rafe Stocker is running things at Wade Manor. I know I can rely on you both to give him your full support. And now — ' Max signalled to the waiter, 'I suggest we eat. After all, we are here to celebrate my birthday.'

2

'The floor is yours,' Max said to Rafe over coffee in the lounge.

'Thank you, Max,' Rafe replied. 'May I first say, I hope your retirement will be a long and happy one, and that you have my assurance that I will do everything to uphold the good image of Wade Manor.'

'That's all very well,' Ben began.

'I believe I gave Rafe leave to speak first,' Max reminded his son. Ben retreated into silence with a scowl.

'I shall of course insist on certain conditions,' Rafe said.

'I rather thought you might.' Max made a wry face, his blue eyes twinkling as if he were enjoying a private joke.

Lunch had been a stilted affair, during which time Max had forbidden anyone to talk business. Stacey had been brimming with questions but, mindful that it was Max's birthday, she contented herself instead with telling him about Emily's party. She had also listened to Rafe talk about Australia and how on the death of his father he had decided to visit the old country to look up some of his old haunts.

It wasn't easy trying to concentrate on what Rafe was saying. Stacey's brain was buzzing with all the news and she was still trying to work out where she had heard mention of Rafe Stocker's name before. Although he was wearing a navy blue blazer, white shirt and grey slacks, Stacey imagined Rafe was more at home surfing the breaker waves on a white sands beach. He had the complexion of a man who preferred to spend his time outdoors rather than in front of a computer screen.

'We moved to Australia when I was a child. My mother likes the life out there and she has decided to stay on, but I had a hankering to return to my roots.'

'I'm sure my children will be agog to learn of your plans,' Max said, sipping his peppermint tea.

'What I have in mind is appointing a second in command.'

'You want to bring someone else in?' Ben pounced on his words.

'You'd better look to your laurels, Stacey,' Max warned her, 'although I have a suspicion Rafe intends you for the post.'

Ben's derisive snort was cut short as Rafe calmly interposed. 'Actually, I do.'

The only sound to break the silence that greeted his words was Rafe stirring his black coffee. Stacey was hardly able to believe she had heard him correctly.

'And if I refuse your offer?' She knew she was sounding childish, but her emotions had taken such a battering she was past caring. Her hair had long since worked itself free from any constriction and she threw the velvet bow onto the coffee table in a gesture of irritation. What did frizzy hair matter when her whole future was at stake?

'Then the deal's off,' was Rafe's reply, his eyes searching her face.

'That's blackmail,' Stacey protested.

'Not at all,' Rafe said in a reasonable tone of voice. 'Without your father — sorry,' he looked across to Ben and corrected himself, 'your stepfather's allowance, you will need to find permanent work. I am offering you a job.'

'I have one already, thank you.'

'Doing what?'

'I'm a freelance customer relations officer.'

'It's not much of a job,' Ben butted in. 'Most of the time she plays at it.'

'And I suppose you don't play at painting?' Max enquired mildly.

'That's different,' Ben insisted.

'If you don't take up Rafe's offer, Stacey,' Max said, 'I'll have to cancel my cruise.'

Stacey felt the colour drain from her face. Her mouth went dry and her throat locked. Max was placing her in an impossible situation, but from the look on his face she suspected he knew exactly what he was doing.

'I thought you held views on women in business.' Stacey tilted her chin at him.

'I do,' he replied, the mischievous glint deepening the blue of his eyes. 'I don't think they should be in charge, but I've no objection to them working under a man's guidance.'

'That statement is outdated, sexist and totally the century before last.'

'In that case,' Rafe interrupted, 'isn't it up to you to prove your stepfather wrong, Stacey?'

'How?'

'By accepting my offer. Continuity is important, and with a member of family still involved in the ongoing day-to-day running of Wade Manor, we won't have to work at regaining the public's confidence.'

'Stacey isn't a member of the family,' Ben said with an edge to his voice.

'She is as much my daughter as you are my son,' Max replied, 'and if you persist in your notion of wanting to paint then there is no one else to take up the cudgels.' Ben eased down the collar of his shirt and undid his tie. Max glared at him, stopping Ben short of actually removing it.

'Are you saying I can still go ahead with my plans to visit Provence?' Ben demanded of Max.

'I'm prepared to fund you for one year, after which if you haven't established yourself then, you're to come home or to make your own way in the world.'

Ben's angry frown disappeared in an instant. 'That's terrific news, Dad. I won't let you down, I promise.'

'If you don't, it'll be a first,' Max observed with a wry smile.

'I take it you've now removed your opposition to Stacey's appointment as my second-in-command?' Rafe enquired of Ben.

'My sister's much better suited to that sort of thing than I am, aren't you, Stace?' he said, trying to coax agreement out of her.

'Looks like it's three against one,'

Rafe murmured in Stacey's ear.

'Very well.' Stacey tossed back her head. 'I accept.'

'Excellent. Now as the party seems to be breaking up, you'd better drive me out to this workshop of yours, Ben,' Max said. 'I want to see what sort of investment I'm taking on.'

'If you could see your way to funding some supplies too, Dad? I'm running out of paints and canvas. It would be cheaper to stock up here before I go.'

'Rafe?' Max turned to him. 'You'll give Stacey a lift home, won't you?'

'I can get a cab.' Stacey tried to retie her bow but it kept slipping off because her hair was so soft.

'I should give up,' Rafe advised her as Ben helped his father with his coat. 'When you're working for me I shall of course expect a more groomed appearance.' His eyes lingered on her missing top button.

'There wasn't time to sew it on,' she attempted to explain.

'There would have been if you hadn't

overslept. That's something else I am going to have to insist on.'

'Sewing on buttons?' Stacey hissed back at him. Rafe was pushing her patience to its limits.

'Getting to work on time. It's very different in the real world and the first lesson you're going to have to learn is that there'll be no lying around in bed until all hours because you had a late night.'

Never had Stacey felt such an urge to rage at a man. She was being punished for a situation that was not of her making, while Ben was getting away with an all-expenses-paid year in Provence.

'I've already explained about that.'

'Ben has.' Rafe had as good as thrown down the gauntlet. To tell him what had really happened would be disloyal to Ben and Max. Besides, she had never been one to tell tales. Stacey would never do anything to upset her stepfather; she loved him too deeply. He was a good man, and if he chose to treat his son to a year in France, there was nothing she could do about it. As Ben had so often pointed out, she wasn't really part of the family.

'Eight o'clock tomorrow morning?' Rafe's voice interrupted her thoughts.

'I'll be there.'

'And another thing,' Rafe went on.

'More rules and regulations?'

'You're out of condition.'

'I beg your pardon?'

'A few early morning jogs should ensure you don't mislay any more buttons because your dress is too tight.'

'We're leaving now,' Max called over.

Forgetting all about Rafe, Stacey ran towards Max and hugged him. Through the jacket of his coat she could feel his bones. Max had lost weight. He'd hardly touched his lemon sole at lunch, taken only a sip or two of wine, and he'd declined dessert.

'I'm going to miss you so much,' she whispered as she snuggled up to him. 'Why didn't you tell me you weren't well?'

'There's nothing wrong with me that a bit of good food, rest and some sunshine won't put right.'

The emotion of the day began to weaken Stacey's defences. Her step-father could be the most infuriating of men, but there was no one she loved more in this world.

He stroked her hair away from her face. 'You're so like your mother.'

'Hardly,' Stacey scoffed.

Iris Wade was the epitome of elegance. Hard as she tried to emulate her, Stacey knew she was far too tall and well-built to ever attain her mother's sense of style.

'She was beautiful and caring — all spiky outside, fighting for every injustice going, but deep down she was as soft as marshmallow. Goodness knows what she ever saw in an old war horse like me.'

'She saw a good man, Max, and she loved you very much.'

'There's not a day goes by that I don't miss her.' He squeezed Stacey's elbow.

Stacey inhaled the peaty smell of his dark wool overcoat. It was far too warm a garment for such a day, but Max didn't seem to notice.

'Time to get on, I think, before we both get too mawkish.' His voice was warm against her ear.

'When are you leaving?'

'Half past eight Wednesday morning.'

'So soon?'

'I suspect that if I don't act immediately I'll change my mind, and I don't think my doctors would approve.'

'You must do as they say,' Stacey insisted. 'If you don't, you'll have me to answer to. And I should warn you, I don't take prisoners.'

'That's my girl.' Max kissed her hair. 'You're going to show me I'm wrong, aren't you?'

'About what?'

'I can tell by the way you're tilting your chin at me.' Max chuckled. 'Women in business?' he prompted.

It was an argument they had had so many times in the past; but no matter how hard Stacey argued her case, Max would not listen to reason. In his opinion women did not have the head or the heart for business.

'One word of advice before you fly off the handle,' her stepfather said.

'I'm listening.'

'Rafe Stocker's a good man. Try to heed his advice occasionally.'

'I'll listen to him,' Stacey promised solemnly, 'the same way I've always listened to you. But if I don't agree with what he says I'll have absolutely no compunction about ignoring his advice.'

'Now why doesn't that surprise me?' Max sighed.

'We'd best get going, Dad.' Ben hovered at his elbow.

'Of course.'

'Bye Stace.' Ben air kissed her ear lobe.

'Ben?' Stacey grabbed his sleeve as he made to turn away.

'What?'

'Does the name Rafe Stocker mean

anything to you?'

'I don't think so. Why do you ask?'

'No reason, but don't you find the situation a bit strange?'

'I couldn't say.' Now that his immediate future was mapped out to his advantage, Ben was displaying no further interest in Wade Manor. His attention had already wandered away from Stacey as he looked towards his father.

'I mean, where does he come from? How did he meet Max? What is their connection with each other?'

'Those are questions you'd better ask him yourself.' Ben shrugged. 'Ready, Dad?'

The two men waved goodbye and made their way out of the restaurant. Stacey looked down at the crumpled wrapping paper on the seat. Max had left his present behind. She picked it up, fighting down a lump in her throat.

'He won't be needing these on a Mediterranean cruise, I suppose,' she said as she hugged the cashmere jumper and golfing trousers to her chest, not daring to look up at Rafe in case he sensed her weakness.

'Why don't you look after them until he comes home?' There was no trace of the hard-hitting businessman about Rafe now. His eyes softened at the corners as he smiled at her. Stacey gave a tight nod of her head.

'I suppose we'd best be going too,' Rafe suggested.

All the other tables had now been vacated and the restaurant was empty. Stacey gathered up her things. Like Ben, her future was a blank canvas. Who knew what it held in store for her?

3

'Your third day and already you're late.'
Rafe cast an angry glance at the wall
clock, which was clicking relentlessly
towards midday.

Stacey gave a small shriek and
dropped her handbag in shock. She
hadn't heard Rafe steal up behind her.
'You said you had a business meeting
this morning.'

'Which was cancelled at the last
minute. What's your excuse?'

Dressed in a formal business suit,
pristine white shirt and discreet silk tie,
there was none of the Bondi Beach
surfer about Rafe today. He looked
the total business professional. Stacey
tugged at her creased blouse. There
hadn't been time to iron it.

'Max was leaving for his cruise,' she
rushed into her explanation. 'I promised to see him off.'

'Correct me if I'm wrong, but wasn't his taxi due at half past eight this morning?'

'Yes, but . . . '

'It's now nearly a quarter to twelve.'

'I would have rung in if I'd known you were going to be here.' Stacey realised she'd said the wrong thing the moment she finished speaking.

'As it was, you thought you'd take advantage of my absence to revert to your old ways. What was it this time, some retail therapy?'

'No. It wasn't like that.'

'I'm sure it wasn't.'

'If you'd give me a chance to explain.'

Rafe's eyes travelled down to the gap where Stacey's blouse still refused to meet her skirt. 'All I have to say is, Max would be so very disappointed.'

'How dare you.' The mention of Max's name inflamed Stacey's hold on her temper. She was slow to anger, but Rafe's attitude was more than she could take. She straightened up and prepared for the confrontation that had been brewing ever since she had first met him.

'I decided to give you a chance to prove to me that you could do a proper day's work. I felt I owed it to your stepfather.'

'In that case,' Stacey spoke slowly and clearly, in order to avoid any further misunderstanding, 'shouldn't we be getting on with things, instead of standing here arguing? Unless you have it in mind to dismiss me?'

A small muscle quivered under Rafe's left eye, the only sign of any emotion on his face. 'My office, ten minutes, and smarten yourself up,' he snapped then strode away from the desk.

Pent up with repressed anger, Stacey banged her bags down on the unmanned reception desk.

The centre had been closed since the beginning of the week, while Rafe took stock of the situation. His work schedule was relentless and it had been after half past ten on both Monday and Tuesday evenings before Stacey had been able to leave.

She hadn't minded working a fifteen-hour day. What had irked her was Ben's behaviour. He had left for France late on Monday, having assured her he had ordered Max's taxi for Wednesday morning and done his father's packing. When the taxi hadn't turned up on time and Max still only had a half-filled suitcase, Stacey realised unless she took prompt action, Max would miss his cruise.

Her stepfather looked pale and tired and, anxious not to distress him further, she had insisted he sit quietly in the lounge after he'd got dressed, while she saw to everything. After a last minute hunt for Max's passport and tickets and other documentation, it was after nine o'clock before they left Stopes Cottage. Coming near to breaking every speed limit on the road driving down to the station, Stacey had managed to bundle Max and his suitcase onto the train with one minute to spare. After tipping the guard to keep an extra-special eye on her stepfather and to see he was put in a taxi at the other end, Stacey had leapt out of the carriage almost as the train was drawing away from the platform.

There hadn't been time to go home and freshen up. Hoping to take a shower at the health centre, Stacey had again driven at breakneck speed to Wade Manor. She had been in too much of a rush to notice anything, but the shiny red paint of Rafe's high-performance saloon car now gleamed at her from its designated parking space by the side entrance, and she realised he must have seen her drive in and come straight round to the front of the building to confront her.

Trying to make some sense of her chestnut hair by dragging a brush through it and fixing it back with a neat butterfly clasp, Stacey straightened her blouse and made sure all her buttons were correctly fastened. Her complexion was too heightened for her liking and there was nothing she could do about her smudged mascara. Rafe did not look as though he were in the mood to wait while she re-applied her make up. She contented herself with a quick application of pink lip gloss before turning back to the desk.

Looking round for her notes, she spotted them and grabbed them up, glad she had left them in some kind of order last night. As she'd been working on her business plan for the centre, she hadn't put out her bedside light until well into the small hours. She hoped her scribbled report would make sense in the cold light of day.

She longed to stifle a yawn but she didn't dare. Rafe would seize on every opportunity to remind her of her shortcomings, and from today she intended to give him no further chance to find fault in any area of her work.

'Sit down.' Rafe barely glanced up from his paperwork. Refusing to be intimidated, Stacey drew up a chair and settled down opposite him. After a few moments Rafe closed the file he had been reading.

'The centre is losing money,' he began.

'I think that was because Max was finding things getting on top of him.'

'It's a pity he didn't have you to rely on to help him then, wasn't it?'

'You know how he feels about women in business,' Stacey began, but Rafe held up a hand to stem her flow.

'Membership levels have been falling. The equipment needs updating and the overall decorative image is very tired. We are going to have to come up with an immediate rescue package to save Wade Manor from permanent closure.'

'I've sketched out a few ideas,' Stacey began.

Rafe waved away her file without looking at it. 'What I have in mind in the short term is a publicity drive. We need to put Wade Manor on the map.'

'I thought perhaps we should cut

back on the services we offer,' Stacey suggested.

'I don't agree with you. In today's business world you can't afford to stand still. You have to expand. If we create a modern, positive and successful image, people will regain their confidence in us. Cutting back is not the answer.'

Stacey blinked at Rafe. So far he hadn't listened to a word she had said. 'I've lived in Normanswood for over sixteen years. It's important to understand how things work around here. Hard selling isn't the answer.'

'Then enlighten me,' Rafe clipped back at her, folding his hands and resting his elbows on the desk.

Stacey gulped. 'Locally there's a mixture of young professionals setting up their first homes and older retired couples, as well as a fair sprinkling of young mothers. They all have different schedules and fitness requirements. What appeals to one group, won't necessarily work for another.'

'Agreed.' Rafe waited for Stacey to continue.

'Publicity would have to be something that would appeal to everyone.'

'Exactly what I had in mind.'

'It's no good pushing for a trendy image. Life down here runs at a slower pace. That's why Normanswood and the surrounding areas are popular with the city types, as well as young mothers. Older people enjoy country walks with their dogs; they belong to book groups and look after their grandchildren. With the younger ones it's a need to unwind after a hectic working week.'

'But they're all members of a caring community, wouldn't you say?'

'Of course.' Stacey frowned at Rafe, not sure where his question was leading.

'St Joseph's,' he said and leaned back in his chair.

'I don't understand.' Stacey frowned at him in confusion.

'My proposal is that we stage a

sponsored mini-marathon in aid of St Joseph's.'

'The children's clinic?'

'You have heard of it?'

'Of course, but I don't see the connection.'

St Joseph's had originally been funded by a wealthy philanthropist who, having no family of his own, had willed his home and fortune to create a care centre for children needing convalescent nursing care in calming and relaxing surroundings. The Victorian house stood in its own grounds, a delightful setting a mile or so outside of Normanswood. Parents were allowed to stay with their children and encouraged to take part in local activities in order to lead as regular a life as possible.

'St Joseph's is a cause that will appeal to all members of the community, young and old alike. They are always in need of funds. We will arrange to sponsor a mini-marathon, all proceeds to go to St Joseph's. From what you say there'll be no shortage of volunteers.

Wade Manor will be the control centre — the hub of things. That way we'll get plenty of people through the doors. We give them a publicity pack, entry forms, details of the marathon and a discounted membership application for the health centre.' Rafe raised his eyebrows at Stacey. 'What do you think?'

Stacey cleared her throat. Much as she hated to admit it, it was a brilliant idea. 'It will mean a lot of work,' she hedged.

'Which is where you come in.'

'Me?'

'I shall want you to lead by example.'

'I'll be happy to help in any way I can.'

'Good,' Rafe responded with a quirky smile. 'Because I meant what I said about your fitness regime.'

'I beg your pardon?'

'That means no more late nights or parties. We'll start tomorrow. You'll be in the forefront of things. It will be up to you to present the right image. By that I mean being on time, a smart appearance and the ability to run the entire length of the marathon with the volunteers.'

'What?' Stacey gaped, appalled at the last suggestion.

'Don't worry,' Rafe added with the suggestion of a smile, 'I'm not thinking of twenty-five miles. Three or four will do. People can choose how much or how little of the proposed route they want to undertake.'

'I can't run a marathon, mini or otherwise,' Stacey objected, remembering how she used to invent sick notes at school to get out of any sort of physical activity.

'That is why first light every morning I want you jogging through the village, delivering leaflets promoting the event. I'll run some up on the computer this afternoon.'

'I don't even own a pair of trainers,' Stacey said in desperation.

'It's all been sorted. I've had T-shirts printed with our logo on them. A representative from the sports shop will be calling round this afternoon to kit you out with all that you'll need. They've expressed interest in the event and have promised us as much assistance as we need. It's to their advantage as well. So things are beginning to roll.'

'It would be quicker to drive round with the leaflets,' Stacey put in, thinking on her feet. 'I'd get to see more people.'

'I don't want you jumping in and out of a car, polluting the atmosphere. This is going to be as green a campaign as possible. I need you to talk to people, get the word out on the street and explain what we're doing, why we need their help, and getting them involved in the project.'

'Will you be jogging along with me?' Stacey demanded.

'I shall be here,' Rafe explained.

'Why? The centre's closed.'

'If we're going to re-vamp our image, we need someone on site.'

'Why does it have to be you?'

'Because in your own words, you understand how things work around here. Wasn't that your sales pitch?'

Stacey stifled a sigh. Why hadn't she thought before opening her mouth?

'I'm the new boy; and what's more, I don't come from round here. I'd have to convince them I'm a nice guy. You wouldn't have to do that. Everyone knows Max. They liked him. He was popular. He was part of the community. They'll want to help you make a success of things in his absence.'

Aware she was breathing as if she had already run a half-marathon, Stacey glared at Rafe. He had an answer for everything.

'It doesn't end there,' he went on.

'What doesn't end where?' Stacey demanded.

'Your fitness programme.'

'My what?'

'We won't be able to afford the professional services of an agency. You need a makeover. People will want to see a slim, fit, well-presented person advertising our product.' Rafe leaned forward, his light brown eyes searching her face. Stacey flushed from the intensity of his gaze. 'Your complexion is suffering from your lifestyle. Your core muscles need toning and you need to re-think your diet.'

'You make it sound as if my life has been one long party.'

'How old are you?' Rafe demanded.

'Twenty-five. How old are you?'

'Since you ask, I'm twenty-eight, and I've worked a lot harder than you to get where I am today. You don't seem to realise how lucky you are. Until now you've enjoyed the privilege of a private allowance and an undemanding life-style. All that is about to change. As far as I can see, instead of being grateful for the chance I am giving you to get your life in some sort of order, all you can do is think up excuses not to put yourself out. Well, that's fine with me. There are plenty of females out there who would be only too pleased to leap into your shoes.'

'If we're into plain speaking,' Stacey raised her voice, 'I love my stepfather very much and there are a few things you should know. After my mother died I was the one who held the family together. Ben was only thirteen. He came to rely on me. So did Max. It was an emotionally draining time but I kept going. After I left college Max did his best to help me financially, but that doesn't mean to say I'm scared of hard work. And to prove it, I'll do all you say.'

'Even at the risk of blisters?' Rafe queried in a teasing voice.

Unaware she had leapt to her feet, Stacey glared down at Rafe. 'Where do we start?' she demanded.

'Here and right now,' he countered back at her.

Looking across the grounds outside Wade Manor, Stacey missed the look of grudging respect in Rafe's eyes. She was too busy thinking how much she would enjoy showing him she was up to any challenge he could throw at her.

4

Stacey pounded along the footpath. It hurt to breathe and the muscles in her legs wondered what on earth she was doing — as indeed did Stacey. If it hadn't been for her grim determination to prove to Rafe she could do this, she would have thrown in the towel.

Her satchel full of promotional leaflets banged against her hip — another reason to keep going. The feedback had been positive and several windows displayed notices advertising the mini-marathon. The telephone never stopped ringing with enquiries about the marathon and when the health club would be re-opening.

Much to Stacey's annoyance, Rafe was proving popular with the locals. Like her stepbrother, Ben, he knew how to turn on the charm.

'I don't believe it,' Stacey's friend

Emily mocked from the comfort of her air-conditioned car as she drew up beside her. 'I'd heard rumours that you were on a health kick, but I never realised things had gone this far. What hold has Rafe Stocker got over you? Tell all.'

'Here.' Stacey thrust a fistful of leaflets through the car's open window. 'I'm sure you can dispose of these.'

Emily's eyes widened as she scanned the notice. 'A mini-marathon. Tell me, is the divine Rafe Stocker taking part?'

'Not so far,' Stacey replied, her jaw tight with suppressed annoyance. Why did everyone think the world of him when she was the one pounding the pavement, doing the donkeywork?

'Think I might enter. The thought of Rafe in a pair of shorts and T-shirt is enough to get my pulses racing.'

'We're doing it for St Joseph's,' Stacey pointed out.

'Whatever.' Emily gave a saucy wink. 'Best get on. Will you be catching up with the crowd tonight in the wine bar, or is this health kick for real?'

'It's for real,' was Stacey's grim reply.

'I give it ten days, a fortnight at most,' Emily trilled as she re-started her engine. 'Bye.'

Stacey's stomach gave an angry grumble. Rafe's early-morning call had dragged her from the depths of sleep. There had been no time to snatch any breakfast apart from a quick cup of tea.

'Why aren't you up?' he had growled down the telephone line.

'Because you kept me working past midnight if you recall,' Stacey retaliated.

'You've had over seven hours' sleep,' Rafe replied, 'if you went to bed the moment you got home of course.'

'If you're checking up on me, I didn't go out to a party. I did come straight home but the dogs were desperate to be let out. I had a pile of washing to do. I needed something to eat and Wilcox isn't well.'

'Don't tell me, he's the butler?'

'He's Max's cat, so I didn't go to bed

the moment I got home.'

'Right, well it's a lovely morning. Off you go. I'll see you about half nine.'

Stacey slammed down the receiver. The man was impossible. She wouldn't have minded so much if he set himself the same high standards, but each morning when she arrived at work, it was to find him sharing early elevenses with either the president of a lady's group, or various representatives from St Joseph's or the sports shop, or just about any other local dignitary he could inveigle into his office and sweet-talk into supporting their project.

The renovation programme was already underway, and by the end of the day Stacey's head ached with the constant hammering and sawing and incessant blaring radios the workmen listened to at all hours.

She had kept to her morning regime of jogging, but she had torn up the light diet the nutritionist had devised for her. There had to be more to life than half a grapefruit for breakfast and a salad lunch, she decided; and as Rafe wasn't holding back on the biscuits, she was going to eat chocolate cake whenever she felt like it. She reasoned that she was using up the calories.

So far there had been no comment from Rafe, not even when he'd caught her indulging in a bacon-and-mayonnaise sandwich at the end of a particularly exhausting day. Stacey hoped her glare was steely enough to quell his objections as she carried on eating her sandwich. With a smile that almost suggested sympathy, he had wished her good night and to her surprise told her not to work on too late.

An elderly man walking his dog raised his hat and with a friendly smile wished Stacey good morning as she loped past him. The postman gave a cheery wave, and a crocodile of schoolchildren giggled and pointed at her from across the road. Stacey grinned back. She supposed she did look a bit of a sight. How people managed to look poised and in control when jogging, she had yet to discover. Her hair was a mess, and due to her inner child she hadn't been able to resist splashing through a puddle. Her legs were now mud-stained and, she had to admit, she hadn't felt so happy in a long time.

Today she was doing one of the new estates that had sprung up when some farmland had recently been developed. She felt a little nervous at the prospect. There had been stories about the rougher element of the community frequenting the area.

'Sorry,' a breathless young mother answered just as Stacey was about to thrust a leaflet through the door. 'We were finishing the washing up. Oh, it's you.'

'Do we know each other?' Stacey faltered. The woman's face wasn't familiar. A young child was clinging to her mother's skirt and peering round at Stacey. Behind a pair of spectacles her little blue eyes widened in shyness.

'I'm Sally Good and this is Melanie,' she introduced herself and her daughter. 'I think what you're doing is wonderful.'

'You do?'

'I was up at St Joseph's yesterday.' Melanie cuddled into her mother's side. 'They've promised us a room after Melanie's treatment, haven't they my pet? It's her eyes.' Sally lowered her voice, then smiling again said, 'That's where I saw your posters and that huge photo of you.'

'Me?' Stacey was now more puzzled than ever.

'It's by the entrance and it's life-sized. You're wearing a floppy hat and a spotty summer dress and you're laughing your head off. It's such a happy picture, everyone was talking about it. That was when one of the staff told us about the mini-marathon. We're going to take part, aren't we, Melanie?'

The little girl nodded and continued to suck her thumb.

'We don't think we'll get very far, but

we'll do our best. I've already got three sponsors on my form and Melanie's teacher has got her class involved. They're doing a project on the proposed route and they're going to walk it on the day of the race. It's really exciting. We're new to the area and we thought people might be a bit stuffy, but you're not, are you? Give me some more leaflets. My husband works in a garage. I'm sure the foreman will hand them out to the customers.'

'That's really very kind of you. Er, this photograph of me,' Stacey began as she emptied out her satchel.

'The manager at St Joseph's said the new man at Wade Manor, Rafe is it? Anyway he asked if he could put it up. Thanks for these. Heavens, is that the time? I must fly.'

Back out on the pavement Stacey took a few moments out to regroup. She remembered now where the photo had been taken. She and Max had been attending a garden party and a rather pompous individual had been made to look very foolish when the microphone wouldn't work properly, and his speech came out as a series of distorted squeaks and whines. She and Max had collapsed into a most undignified fit of the giggles. But how had Rafe got hold of it? And why hadn't he mentioned anything to her?

She took a deep breath of fresh morning air. It tingled through her veins. Working out in the open was so much better than the artificiality of an air-conditioned office block. Many were the times she had looked out of tinted windows wishing she didn't feel like a goldfish in a huge glass bowl. Her skin now glowed from all the exercise Rafe had forced on her; and because she no longer spent her evenings in the stuffy confines of restaurants and bars, her hair shone with health.

Stacey's stomach gave another reminding rumble that it still hadn't had its breakfast. She headed towards a bakery she had spotted on the corner of the block. As it came in sight, the enticing smell of freshly baked bread lured her onwards. The small queue outside shuffled slowly forward.

'What's that about, then?' A shaven-headed youth pointed at Stacey's T-shirt as he swaggered towards her. The black military vest he was wearing exposed his tattooed arms.

'We're sponsoring a mini-marathon,' she began to explain.

'Waste of time.'

'No it isn't,' Stacey protested.

'Bet you're gonna make off with all the money yourself.'

Stacey's feelgood factor evaporated. Casting wary glances in her direction, the bakery queue began to edge away from the pair of them.

'Would you mind repeating that comment?' Stacey demanded.

'You heard,' the youth mumbled.

'I wasn't sure I heard you correctly.' Stacey raised her voice. 'I believe you accused me of taking money from innocent people in the name of charity and keeping it for myself?'

'Everyone knows Max Wade couldn't make a go of things.' The youth began to look a little unsure of his ground. 'What makes you think you'll do any better?'

'I don't know but at least I'm trying.'

'Says you.'

'What are you doing with your day, apart from lounging around outside a bakery? You look fit enough to work to me.' Stacey refused to be intimidated by his sneer or the size of his knuckles, which he began to flex. They made an alarming cracking noise.

'This isn't your patch. Get back up the posh end of town and take your leaflets with you.'

A military-looking gentleman appeared by Stacey's side. Before she could protest, he snatched up her satchel and thrust a wad of leaflets at the biker.

'I suggest, young man, that you and that crowd of yours sign up right now. You hear me? And we want no more remarks about Miss Oliver making off with the proceeds. That's slander, and I am a local magistrate so I know what I'm talking about. Do I make myself clear?'

The youth was now seriously out-numbered, his belligerent expression giving way to one of unease. 'I only said . . . '

'We all heard what you 'only said'. Now sign up for the run.'

'Bacon roll, was it, love? Here, on the house.' The baker, fed up with standing behind her counter and getting no response from her customers, had strolled outside. She handed Stacey a warm filled paper bag. 'Anything that gets that lot away from my shop front is worth a freebie. A bit of running will do them the world of good.'

'Captain Jones, ex-army. You can call me Sidney,' Stacey's new friend intro-duced himself as the youth shuffled away. 'Hope that little scene didn't distress you too much, only I couldn't stand by and listen to him insulting a lady.'

'No, I'm sorry I started it really,' Stacey apologised.

'Nonsense. Now eat your breakfast before that bacon gets cold.'

Perching on the little wall outside the shop, Stacey licked grease off her fingers. She had delivered every leaflet, and Captain Jones — Sidney — had made off with the last of her sponsorship forms. Raising her face to the sunshine as it peeped out from behind a fluffy white cloud, Stacey let its rays play on her face. In the distance she heard car tyres splashing through the recent rain puddles. She stood up with a reluctant sigh. Some drivers weren't too careful how they drove and more than once had splashed her legs with cold muddy water as they sailed past.

She began a slow jog back to Wade Manor. The approaching car overtook her. With the sun against it the paintwork looked black, but as it slowly turned the corner and disappeared into the shade she saw it was a red saloon. Rafe was at the steering wheel. He gave a cheery wave as he spotted her in his rear-view mirror. Outraged that he hadn't stopped to give her a lift, Stacey paused, hands on hips. As she was debating whether or not it would be dignified to call after him she noticed his passenger, a cool honey-blonde, who after a quick glance in Stacey's direction turned her attention back to Rafe. She whispered something in his ear. Moments later, with a quick glance in her direction, they both began to roar with laughter.

5

'If you want to drive around the countryside with a blonde companion at your side, making jokes at my expense, then carry on, but don't expect me to enjoy the experience.'

Stacey had trouble controlling her breathing she was so annoyed. After Rafe had swept past her and his car had disappeared into the distance she had broken all jogging records getting back to Wade Manor. Looking at the expression on Rafe's face now, she was sorely tempted to twirl her empty satchel in the air like a lasso and rope him in like a branded steer. She wondered how funny he would find it to be held up as an object of ridicule. 'How adult is that?' she demanded. 'You're no better than a schoolboy.'

'Helena is a business colleague.'

'First-name terms already?' Stacey

arched an eyebrow. 'I hope *Helena's* signed up for a spot of jogging. I expect she would look quite glamorous in a cutesy singlet and shorts.'

'Stacey, listen to me,' Rafe attempted to interrupt. He had been pacing the steps outside reception, waiting for her. She shook his hand off her arm with an angry twist of her wrist.

'Not now, Rafe.'

'We need to talk.'

'I need to freshen up.'

'There's been a telephone call for you. A French woman has been trying to get hold of you. I couldn't understand all she was saying but it sounded important. You'd better ring her back.'

'Ben's in France.' Stacey blinked at Rafe.

'Use the landline. We don't want the signal going down in the middle of your call.' He squinted at his scribbled note. 'Madame Joffré?' Stacey could hear the torrent of French coming back at him. 'Moment, please. I have, er, *ici*

Mademoiselle Oliver.' He thrust the telephone at her. 'Can you speak French?'

'Well enough to get by.' Stacey grabbed the receiver from him. There followed several moments of agitated conversation. 'It's Max,' she said after she finished the call.

'What's wrong with him?' Rafe demanded.

'They tried to get hold of Ben because Max put his name down as next of kin.' A sob rose in Stacey's throat. 'Mahon is in Menorca isn't it?' she asked between gulps.

'Sit down before you collapse.' Rafe pushed Stacey towards a chair. 'Wait here,' he ordered. He was back in a short space of time with a flask. 'I managed to snaffle this off one of the workmen.'

Stacey pulled a face. 'I don't drink sweet tea,' she protested as her teeth vibrated against the plastic cup.

Rafe grabbed a towel to mop up the mess. 'Now, tell me what's happened.'

'Ben was staying with Madame Joffré, but he's moved out and he didn't leave a forwarding address. She found my number amongst some papers he left behind so she called me. I couldn't understand all she was saying, but Max was taken off the ship in Menorca and I think he's in hospital. I have to fly out there.'

An incoming text on Rafe's mobile interrupted them. He read it with a gesture of annoyance.

'Can I help?' a female voice enquired.

'Helena.' Rafe greeted the new arrival in relief. 'Can you see to Stacey for me? She's had some bad news.'

'Of course.'

'I've got that party of VIPs to show round and I'm late. They're wondering what's happened to me. I can't keep them waiting any longer.'

'Don't worry. You go; I'll look after Stacey.'

'You're Rafe's passenger.' Stacey shrank from Helena's touch. 'The business friend who laughed at me.'

'I did no such thing,' Helena insisted.

'I saw you, with Rafe.'

'We'll discuss it later. Right now you need a hot shower.'

'I can look after myself, thank you.' Stacey knew she was behaving badly but Helena was the last person in this world from whom she was going to accept help.

'I'll find you some fresh clothes.' Unperturbed by her outburst, Helena gave her a generous smile that made Stacey feel like an ungrateful brat. 'One of the workmen has managed to get shower number three in decent working order.' Helena propelled her towards it. 'I'll leave you to it.'

When Stacey emerged, the warm water having revived her, she found a pair of jogging pants and a warm sweater on the stool outside. 'I can't wear these,' she protested when Helena popped her head round the door.

'Why not?'

'Rafe operates a strict business code in the club even though we're not yet open to the public.'

'I'll deal with Rafe if he starts anything,' Helena replied.

'That's my job.'

'Then we'll job share.' A dimple deepened in Helena's cheek.

Given other circumstances, Stacey decided she would have liked Helena. Underneath the blonde femininity Stacey suspected she was a tough cookie. 'We didn't get off to a good start, did we?' she thrust her head through the neck of the sweater.

'Then why don't we start again?' Helena responded with a twinkle in her eye. 'Sidney Jones is a neighbour of mine and the sight of him confronting an oily biker struck me as funny. The boy was at least six inches taller then him and a good forty years younger, but Sidney wasn't in the least bit intimidated. He's gone up in my estimation. Until now, to be honest, I've always thought him a bit pompous.'

'Don't you knock Sidney. He was my knight errant.'

'They come in all shapes and sizes, so they say.'

Both girls broke into spontaneous smiles. Stacey was used to making on-the-spot character judgements. She decided she liked Helena. 'I'm Stacey Oliver.' She held out her hand. 'In case you don't already know, Max Oliver is my stepfather.' Mention of Max's name caused Stacey's heartbeat to quicken.

'Helena Carter, your new receptionist,' Helena replied.

'What?' Stacey's resentment of the girl resurfaced.

'Didn't Rafe tell you?' Helena raised her eyebrows in surprise.

'No, he didn't.'

'Honestly, men are hopeless. Can we talk about the appointment later?' Helena suggested. 'I don't know what's happened but Rafe said something about Max being taken ill?'

Stacey's bacon roll churned in her stomach as she recalled her telephone conversation with Madame Joffré. 'I need to go online and check the flights to Mahon.'

'I already did,' Helena explained. 'There's a flight leaving from Gatwick in two hours. I've booked you a seat. I hope I did the right thing. All you have to do is get there.'

'Thanks. I'm on my way.' Stacey snatched up her bag and keys.

'You won't be going anywhere in that.' One of the workmen strolled by Stacey's car. 'Flat tyre,' he said, pointing out the obvious. Stacey stared at it in dismay.

'Want a lift in my van?' he offered.

'That won't be necessary. I'll get Miss Oliver to the airport in time for her flight,' a clipped voice interrupted them.

'What about your VIPs?'

'Helena's dispensing coffee and biscuits. When they run out she says she'll think of something else to do. Now get in.' Rafe eased his car out into the road.

'Why didn't Max tell us he wasn't well?'

'He's a tough old bird. He doesn't like admitting to weakness. It goes with the territory.'

'If anything's happened to him . . . ' Stacey squeezed the tissue Helena had given her. It was now a soggy ball.

'He'll be fine,' Rafe assured her. 'I expect when you get out there he'll be sitting up in bed demanding to know what all the fuss is abut.'

'I'm sure he'll be insisting he doesn't want any females bossing him about. He is such a dinosaur when it comes to women. He thinks we can't cope without a man's protection. It used to drive my mother mad. She was an independent lady, yet Max treated her as though she couldn't cross the road safely without a male escort.'

'That's because he loved her.' The sideways look Rafe cast in Stacey's direction caused a hot flush to stain her cheeks. 'Normanswood. We're here. Where do I go now?' Rafe said.

'Lavender Lane's impassable. The potholes are too deep for cars.'

Rafe drew into a parking space outside a shoe shop. 'Hurry up then; I'll keep the engine running. Don't forget your passport.'

The smell of kerosene grew stronger and jets roared overhead as Stacey spotted the airport buildings in the distance.

'Ben,' she gasped. 'He's got to be told. Madame Joffré said he moved out about ten days ago.'

'Leave all that to me. I'll track him down. A word of advice,' he added before Stacey could unlock the door as he came to a halt. 'Whatever Max says, he'll be depending on you, so don't stand any nonsense from him.'

'I intend to give him what-for,' Stacey said with a bravado she was far from feeling. She grabbed up her bag and strode towards the check-in desks.

'I think there's been some mistake,' Stacey advised the purser as she boarded the aircraft and was guided towards the business class seats. 'My ticket is a last-minute instant saver.'

'Mr Stocker is one of our frequent flyers, so he enjoys certain privileges,' the purser replied. 'Would you like a window seat? The flight isn't full so you can spread out.'

Too exhausted to protest, Stacey sank into the comfortable seat and closed her eyes. In the background she heard the whine of the aircraft engines. The next moment she felt a bump and she realised with a shock that the aircraft had landed at Mahon Airport.

6

Stacey caught a taxi from the airport to the centre of Mahon where the offices of the cruise company's agent were situated.

'You'll need this.' Rafe had thrust a note of the address into Stacey's hands as she jumped out of the car. 'I looked it up and rang them while you were collecting your things at the cottage,' he explained. 'A Luis Santos will be expecting you.'

The office was on the third floor of a building situated up a steep side street, away from the hustle and bustle of the area around the fish market.

Stacey had expected the weather to be warmer. The weak sunshine was being beaten away by a cold wind from the east. Many of the shops were still shuttered for the winter and there were few tourists about.

71

'Season, too early,' her driver said with his limited command of English as she settled the fare. 'Two weeks, you come back for sunshine.'

A black-clad olive-seller indicated to Stacey that she should proceed up the stairs of the dismal-looking building. From a pantomime of gestures Stacey understood the offices to be on the left at the top of the staircase. Her footsteps echoed on the stone-flagged floor as she entered the building. She shivered again. The thick stone dropped the temperature even further.

'Stacey Wade?' The door was half open and a dark-haired man leapt to his feet at the sound of her tentative knock. 'I am Luis Santos,' he introduced himself. '*Bienvenido* to Menorca.'

'Thank you, and it's Stacey Oliver,' Stacey corrected him.

'*Si*, of course.'

'Max Wade is my stepfather.'

'Your husband, he explain to me.'

'I don't have a husband.'

Luis frowned and looked down at a

piece of paper on his desk. 'Sorry. I receive a message from my colleague. What can I do to help you? Please take a seat. Would you like some coffee, or perhaps tea?'

'Nothing, thank you. I'm here because I understand my stepfather was taken off his cruise ship due to ill health.'

'That is correct. The captain arranged for an ambulance to take him to the municipal hospital. Unfortunately the cruise ship only docked for a short while and has already left, so you will be unable to speak to the captain, but I have all the details.'

'What happened?'

'Señor Wade felt unwell. I will drive you to the hospital if you wish. You speak Spanish?' Luis asked.

'No.' Stacey shook her head.

'In that case you will need my help. Shall we go?'

Stacey's sleep on the aircraft had done little to clear her muzzy head. The cabin crew had insisted she drink some water on landing to keep up her fluid levels, as she had taken nothing during the flight. They had also pressed on her a small bag of barley sugars to suck. She took the bag out of her bag now and offered one to Luis. They sucked in silence for a few moments.

'Here we are,' Luis announced as they drove through the entrance. 'I will go and see what has happened.'

'I'm coming with you,' Stacey insisted, wishing now she had thought to bring a few overnight essentials for Max. She imagined there wouldn't have been time to pack his bags off the cruise ship and he would need basic necessities.

'He's not here,' Luis said after a swift exchange with one of the administrators on the desk.

'Then where is he?' Stacey demanded, her panic levels rising again.

'He discharged himself.'

'What?'

'Do you know a Mrs Dolly Travers?' Luis looked questioningly at Stacey.

'I've never heard of her.'

'She came to visit him and said she would take him home. I have her address. Would you like me to take you there?'

'Very much indeed.' Stacey's panic was now turning to annoyance. She was beginning to feel she had been the victim of a wild goose chase.

'She lives in a villa a few kilometres to the south of the island. Casa Maria it is called. Mary's house?'

Stacey nodded, her limited knowledge of Spanish having grasped the rough translation.

'They tell me on the desk that Mrs Travers is an English lady who has lived out here many years.'

'She had no right to remove my stepfather without the family's permission.'

'Mr Wade did not go unwillingly. He did not like being in the hospital and he insist that he is fit enough to leave.' Luis smiled. 'You're looking tired. Why don't you relax while I drive you to this

Mary's House? Save your energy for Mrs Travers.'

The deep blue of the Mediterranean stabbed the back of Stacey's eyes as Luis drove along the coastline. At any other time Stacey would have enjoyed the views across the water as the sun cast contrasting light and shadow over the harbour. She'd read somewhere that there was much evidence of the former British occupation of the island. They had already passed what looked like former fortifications left over from its chequered past.

'Here we are,' Luis announced as he completed a sharp turn and came to a halt. 'I cannot drive any further. The cove is only accessible from the house.' They had drawn up outside a sturdy wooden gate. A crazy-paving path led down to a white-painted villa, built in a typical Moorish style. 'It's a nice property. These villas are very exclusive. They have private access to the beaches and their own pools. It looks like your stepfather has done well for himself.

Does he play golf?'

'What?' Stacey wasn't really listening to Luis. She was busy wondering exactly what Mrs Travers would be like. 'Sorry, yes, he does,' she replied, realising she was being less than polite.

'There is a course close by and a club house. I can understand why Mr Wade did not want to stay in the hospital. This is much nicer.'

'Thank you for the lift.' Stacey opened her passenger door.

'I'll wait if you like?' Luis produced a newspaper from the back seat. 'You go and find Mrs Travers.'

Bright scarlet blossoms tumbled out of white boxes at the open windows. Bougainvillea trailed down the white painted walls and several cats dozed in the sun. Stacey hoped Rafe would remember to see to Wilcox and to ask Emily to look after Lord and Lady. The dogs were highly strung and would pine if they didn't see a face they recognised. Why was Ben never available in an emergency? He was always pointing out that Max was his father, yet he was never around to help with the really heavy stuff.

Stacey tugged at a large iron bell pull by the wooden front door. In the background she could hear voices and the splash of water and what sounded like the chink of glasses. When there was no reply she indicated to Luis that she was going to try round the back.

'Hello?' she called out. 'Is anybody there?'

'Hi,' a female voice replied. 'Come on through.'

Max was stretched out on a sun bed under an enormous sunshade. Although there was a brisk breeze, he was wearing a brightly coloured pair of beach shorts and a huge straw hat. He was clutching a glass of fruit juice and sharing a joke with a white-haired lady, impeccably clad in brilliant blue Capri pants and matching shirt.

Stacey charged towards the pair of them and, forgetting all manners, demanded of Max, 'Just exactly what do you think you're doing?'

Max sat bolt upright, spilling his drink. 'Blast. Dolly, bring me something to wipe up the mess would you, darling?'

His companion was already on hand with a roll of kitchen towel.

'You're supposed to be ill. I get frantic telephone calls about you from Ben's French landlady. I race out here to discover you refuse to stay in hospital. I finally track you down lazing around in a deck chair, drinking cocktails and flirting with a female who you call darling.'

Dolly was the first to break the stunned silence. Her voice was low and her smile friendly. 'You must be Stacey? I do apologise. What a shock you must have had. Now, first of all, I am Dolly Travers. I'm a perfectly respectable widow. My late husband was a friend of Max's. When I got Max's call, I hared down to the hospital. I was so pleased to see him again and well, darling, you see, life at the Casa Maria gets a bit lonely now I live here on my own, and when Max hinted that he hated hospitals, I suggested he came here. We thought we'd sit by the pool for a while and have a bit of a siesta. If I'd known you were coming I'd have driven down to the airport to meet you.'

'Dolly, pipe down, there's a love,' Max interjected.

'Heavens,' Dolly giggled, 'I always talk too much when I'm nervous.'

'Yes, you do,' Max agreed with her. 'Stacey, how did you get out here?'

'From Gatwick,' Stacey began.

'I mean here, to the Casa Maria.'

'Luis Santos drove me up from the agent's office via the hospital. He's still parked outside. He said he would wait for me.'

'You must spend the night here,' Dolly insisted. 'Would you like me to have a word with Luis? Why don't I leave you two together to have a private talk?' Dolly beamed at Stacey. 'I love young people. Harvey and I never had a family of our own.' Still twittering,

Dolly drifted away with the empty drinks jug.

'Sit down,' Max said in a softer voice, adding, 'I'll forgive you for your outburst this time because I realise you are under pressure, but don't ever speak like that to Dolly again.'

'What did you expect me to do?' Stung by the unfairness of Max's remark, Stacey dragged another deck chair over and flopped down into it.

'Show some good manners?' Max suggested.

'I didn't mean to be rude, Max, but Ben's landlady said something about your heart and hospital. I was out of my mind with worry.'

'Where is that son of mine?' Max demanded.

'I don't know,' Stacey admitted. 'Rafe's going to see if he can track him down. He's moved from the address he gave you.' Stacey flapped her hands. 'Never mind all that. How are you?'

'Fit as a fiddle. To be honest I was finding life on board a bit boring.

Whenever I settled down for a quiet read I was pestered by elderly ladies of a certain age. They wanted to engage me in conversation or teach me bridge or get me to join an exercise class. By day two I'd had enough.'

'What about the chest pains?' Stacey interrupted him.

A guilty look crossed Max's face. 'I didn't feel too bright and I think it might have been the seafood salad. I've always had a bit of an allergy to shellfish. Anyway, the next thing I know is the captain's had me disembarked and parked up at the local hospital. I know I wanted to get off the wretched ship but putting me in hospital I thought was going a step too far. Anyway, the idea suddenly came to me.'

'What idea?'

'Dear old Dolly and Harvey. We always exchange cards at Christmas and I had her number in my wallet so I gave her a call and to cut a long story short, here I am.'

'What do you intend to do now?'

'Dolly has very kindly issued an open invitation so I think I'll stay on for a while. After all, the doctors prescribed lots of rest and a warm climate and Dolly assures me the sun will be hotting up soon, so there you have it.' Max squeezed Stacey's fingers.

'I thought,' Stacey's voice gave out on her. She rubbed her nose vigorously with one of Dolly's tissues. 'I'm not crying,' she insisted.

'Yes you are,' Max said gently, then added with a teasing tone to his voice, 'I told you women get over-emotional.'

'That remark is below the belt, Max,' Stacey retaliated.

Her stepfather had the grace to look shamefaced. 'I'm sorry. It's my way of saying I'm so pleased to see you. I know I've behaved irresponsibly and I don't deserve you as a stepdaughter, but why don't you give me one of your special hugs and we'll say no more about it?'

When Dolly emerged onto the terrace clutching a newly refilled jug of peach juice a few moments later, it was to find Stacey with her arms around Max's neck.

'Careful, you two,' she called over. 'That sun bed is decidedly wonky and I don't want to have to retrieve you both from the pool, especially as I'm not a very good swimmer.' She put her jug down on a side table. 'There now, we're all friends again. I am so looking forward to doing girly things with you, Stacey. You will stay on for a few days, won't you? I've asked Fiorella, my maid, to make up a bed, and I'm not taking no for an answer, so it's pointless you giving me some nonsense about having to fly back immediately.'

It was only as Stacey was slipping between cool cotton sheets late in the evening after a delicious meal of watermelon, followed by sea bass, that she remembered in all the excitement she had forgotten to telephone Rafe. Too exhausted to do anything about her lapse at this late hour, she fell asleep the moment her head touched the pillow.

7

'Why don't we go out for a drive and take in lunch at a lovely fish restaurant I used to go to with Harvey?' Dolly was again impeccably dressed. This morning she was wearing tailored lemon slacks and a tangerine top. After ascertaining that Stacey had slept well, she set about organising their day.

'Nothing too strenuous of course. My poor old boy couldn't be doing with that, could you?' Dolly fussed over Max and Stacey couldn't help noticing the rapport between them. Max had never been much of a one for the ladies. Even after her mother died she couldn't remember him with any particular female. She wondered how far back the relationship went between himself and Dolly.

'Why don't you wear that new shirt I bought you?' Dolly suggested to Max, adding for Stacey's benefit, 'I had to go on an emergency shopping trip. He only had the clothes he stood up in. Max's suitcase and the rest of his belongings are probably halfway to the Greek Islands by now.'

'Good idea. I shouldn't be seen out in public in these shorts.' Max got slowly to his feet and cleared his throat. 'It's lovely to have you here, Stacey,' he said, like a child reciting a lesson. 'Thank you for coming. I'm sorry I caused you so much trouble.'

'I told him to say that,' Dolly confided when Max was out of earshot.

Stacey sipped her coffee. It was hot and strong and began to revive her flagging senses. She hadn't expected to get a wink of sleep after such a traumatic day, but she hadn't woken up until there was a gentle tap on her door and Fiorella asked if Stacey would like her to run a bath. It had taken Stacey a few moments to remember where she was and all that had happened the day before.

'Take as much time as you like, darling.' Dolly appeared behind Fiorella and poked her head round the bedroom door. 'Max is resting. No hurry at all.'

With her spirits revived by a lemon-scented soak in the bath, Fiorella had pointed Stacey towards the terrace. Dolly had greeted her with an enthusiastic kiss on both cheeks and immediately put down the secateurs she was using to trim the dead leaves on a rose bush.

'That stepfather of yours takes too much for granted.' Dolly nudged a basket of rolls towards Stacey. 'And as for Ben, best not get me started there.'

Stacey buttered a roll and coated it with honey. 'Mmm.' she wiped at her lips with a paper napkin, unable to stop herself saying, 'What delicious honey.'

'I get it from the nuns. There's a convent not far away and they keep bees,' Dolly explained. 'I think it's the clover that gives it that special taste. Actually,' Dolly tapped Stacey on the arm and looked over her shoulder as if checking there was no on around to over hear. 'I engineered that little scene with Max to get him out of the way, because I want to have a private word with you.'

'We do need to talk about Max,' Stacey admitted, having finished her second roll. 'Sorry, I can't believe I've been so greedy.' She looked at her empty plate.

'I must say you look better after a night's sleep. You poor lamb, what you must have been through.'

'I don't believe I've thanked you properly.' Stacey's smile was a tad on the shaky side. Dolly's concern was attacking her emotions at their most vulnerable.

Dolly waved away her thanks. 'Not necessary. What I want to say is I've loved having Max here. I'm the type of female who likes to have a man about the place. You know, someone to tell me how lovely I look and to have dinner with, that kind of thing. I'm not vain, don't get me wrong; just a bit of a peacock I suppose. Harvey was a wonderful husband and he understood my needs. His loss has left a huge gap in my life.'

'Are you saying you want Max to fill that gap?' Stacey still didn't quite know what to make of Dolly.

'Let's cross that bridge when we come to it.' Dolly looked at her expectantly. 'For the moment I'd like him to stay. The doctors want to see him again and I can drive him to and from various appointments. So there you have it. There isn't much else to tell you I'm afraid. I suppose I must have been a bit of a shock to you?'

'I have to say I was wondering what I would find out here,' Stacey admitted. 'I mean I've never heard of you. Sorry,' she apologised, 'that sounded rude.'

'Not at all. I owe you an explanation, and in your position I would probably have felt exactly the same. I'll tell you a little about myself, shall I? Harvey and I lived in America for a long time. When Harvey retired we decided to come here to live. The climate suited his health.

He liked the sun and the relaxed lifestyle. I'm not sure exactly how he and Max knew each other, but they were typical men and never bothered much to keep in touch. That was in the days before computers when communication meant writing a letter or making a telephone call. The two men did exchange cards at Christmas and that was about the sum of things.'

'You don't have to tell me all this,' Stacey protested, feeling slightly embarrassed by Dolly's openness and her own earlier suspicions.

'It's important to me, darling. I want you to understand that Max's happiness is my only motivation.'

'If Max is happy, then so am I,' Stacey replied.

Dolly's bright smile lit up her face. 'I knew you'd understand. Max has told me all about you. He is so proud of you, you know, but I'm speaking out of turn.' Dolly went pink. 'Hush up, here he comes. Don't you look smart in your new clothes!' She waved at Max.

Stacey looked down at the sundress she was wearing. There hadn't been time to pack much in the way of essentials. The dress was crumpled but she had nothing else to hand.

'I've put a T-shirt and skirt out on your bed,' Dolly said. 'They might be warmer than your dress, pretty though it is.' She added, 'That colour does bring out the hazel lights in your eyes, doesn't it, Max?'

Unused to being asked for his opinion in matters of fashion, Max looked at Stacey with a wry smile. 'You took the very words out of my mouth, Dolly,' he replied.

'If you'd like to leave your dress out, Stacey, Fiorella will launder it for you. Now how are you for toiletries? I've plenty of make-up too. Just help yourself.'

Their drive had taken them to a small fishing port tucked away on the south of the island. A few exclusive yachts were moored in the harbour. The water slapped lazily against their brightly painted hulls.

'One of the island's best kept-secrets,' Dolly told Max and Stacey as they picked their way down a flight of steps to the marina. A striped awning sheltered lunchtime diners from the heat of the sun. 'Harvey discovered it on one of his jaunts and we always came here every Sunday. Mario,' she air kissed one of the waiters, 'it's good to see you again. I've bought two of my best friends to sample your dish of the day. Do you have a table for us? Something inside I think. Mr Wade needs to stay out of the sun.'

Max slipped his fingers through Stacey's. 'Best let her have her head,' he murmured. 'It's what Dolly does best — organising people. We'll have a quiet word together later. By the way, that little speech I made this morning? I really meant every word. I know I can be a stubborn old nuisance at times.'

'You've always been a stubborn old nuisance,' Stacey agreed with him, 'but that's the way you are and I wouldn't have things any different. And,' she added, 'I approve of Dolly.'

'It looks like we're under starters orders.' Max nudged Stacey towards a window table. 'Dolly appears to have wangled us the best seats in the house.'

* * *

Gentle waves lapped the sand as Max and Stacey strolled along the shore.

'Need a bit of exercise to work off that lunch,' Max said, taking a deep breath. 'Dolly certainly knows how to talk too. My head is still spinning.'

In accordance with local custom, lunch had gone on until well in the afternoon. Dolly had driven them back to her villa; then, pleading a prior engagement with a friend, had gone out again almost immediately, leaving Max and Stacey alone.

'You did mean what you said about liking Dolly, didn't you?'

'I like her very much,' Stacey said.

Over lunch Dolly had proved to be warm-hearted and well thought of by various friends who stopped by their table to have a brief word. Dolly lost no opportunity to introduce them all to Stacey and Max as her very dear friends from England.

'I'm thinking of staying on, you see,' Max confided.

'Dolly said she thought you might.'

'You had a little chat about me, didn't you? It's all right, I don't mind,' Max assured her. 'I suspected something of the sort when she sent me off to get rigged up in this rather expensive shirt. What do you think of it?' Max extended his arms and did half a twirl.

'It's not really you is it?' Stacey said after a short pause.

'My thoughts exactly,' Max agreed with her. 'I mean, sky-blue pink?'

Stacey giggled. 'You do look a bit . . . ' she searched around for the right word.

'Don't say it,' he implored, 'and for goodness sake don't mention anything to Dolly. I wouldn't hurt her feelings for the world.'

'You have my word,' Stacey agreed.

'I'll have to go along with her next time she has a shopping spree in mind.'

'You've really made up your mind to stay then?'

'I thought I would for a while. Dolly has lots of friends and I can have my own set of rooms in the villa. We don't have to meet up if we don't want to, but we'd be company for each other and like Dolly, I have been lonely of late. You are all right with it?'

'Go for it, Max.' Stacey squeezed his fingers.

'Bless you.' He kissed her fingers.

'But make sure you take things easy.'

'I will.'

'Dolly strikes me as a lady who might get easily carried away. I wouldn't want you doing too much.'

'Promise. Now, change of subject. Rafe Stocker?'

'What about him?' Stacey asked guardedly.

'How are things between you?'

'We're rubbing along. We — ' Stacey

gasped. 'Oh my goodness. I was supposed to telephone him when I arrived, but in all the chaos, I forgot.'

'You can do it when we get back,' Max reassured her. 'He'll know that if it was anything serious you would have been in touch before now.'

'Is Rafe Stocker another old friend from your past?' Stacey asked.

'His father was.' Max gazed out to sea and carried on talking as if he had forgotten Stacey was there. 'I felt so bad when the money went missing. I shouldn't have accused Anthony of being involved but in those days I was a bit of a hothead. I couldn't see who else it could have been. He had the combination to the safe and access to all the accounts. It was only later I found out it wasn't him, but by then the damage had been done.'

'I thought the name Stocker was familiar to me.' Stacey began to remember an old scandal from about the time her mother had started seeing Max on a regular basis. She'd never really known the details, and after it had all blown over Max never mentioned the name again.

Max came back to the present with a start. 'It's old history. Forget I mentioned it. The thing is, I wanted Rafe to be involved in the running of Wade Manor to make up for my unfounded suspicions about his father. That's why it's important to me that the two of you get along. You will try, won't you?'

'You could have mentioned something before your birthday. It was such a shock when you sprung it on us.'

'That's the way I like to operate,' Max said with a trace of his old business style.

'Why can you never trust me?' Stacey demanded.

'Yoo-hoo.'

Look, there's Dolly,' Max said, a note of relief in his voice, 'and she's waving a plate of ensaimadas at us from the terrace. Where on earth did she get those? You've got to try them. They are absolutely delicious. Lethal for the waistline, all that dough coated in cream, jam and almonds, but we can't disappoint, her can we? That wretched doctor at the hospital mentioned something about a diet, but I wasn't having any of that. Come on. Let's go and indulge ourselves. All that walking has revived my appetite.'

'It's Ben on the phone,' Dolly said in a low voice later in the evening when she and Stacey were enjoying the sunset on the terrace. 'I don't want to wake Max. Will you have a word with him?'

Stacey drew her eyes reluctantly away from the vermilion and purple lights in the sky and headed indoors.

'Found you at last,' Ben greeted her. 'You've no idea the trouble I've had tracking you down. Goodness knows how many telephone calls I've made. What's going on?'

'It would have been helpful if you'd told us you'd moved.'

'That's not an answer to my question.'

Stacey sighed. Arguing with Ben would not do the situation any good. 'Max is fine. He's decided to leave the cruise and stay on in Menorca for a while.'

'The message I got was that he was ill and that he'd been carted off to hospital.'

'It was a touch of food poisoning.' Stacey skated round the details.

'Is that all?' Ben now sounded full of outrage.

'You should be glad it's nothing more serious.'

'Of course I am, but if it's not serious why on earth did you go haring out there?'

'Like you, I didn't know what was happening.'

'I got all sorts of garbled messages.'

'So did I,' Stacey replied, doing her best to keep her voice steady. There were times when Ben could be very selfish.

'Who's the female who answered the phone?' he demanded.

'Dolly Travers. She and her husband were old friends of Max's. Dolly's a widow.'

'I don't like the sound of this. I think I'd better have a word with Dad.'

'He's asleep.'

'Are you deliberately preventing me from talking to my father?' Ben sounded as though he didn't believe her.

'Nothing of the kind. Look, give me your new number and I'll pass it on to Max and get him to call you as soon as he can. How's the painting going by the way?'

Stacey's mind wandered as her diversion tactic worked and Ben went into a detailed description of all that he had been doing. His concern over Max seemed to have been displaced by his own self-interest, as he told Stacey the reason he had moved was because there was a new female in is life.

'She lived a bit far away from my village, so she found me a place nearer to her parents' house. We're thinking of going into business together.'

'Good. Well, lovely to hear from you,' Stacey said.

'Make sure you keep in touch,' Ben managed to get in as Stacey finished the call.

After checking with Dolly that it was all right to use her telephone again as her mobile had run out of charge, Stacey dialled Rafe's personal number. She knew he'd taken temporary accommodation in a flat above a shop in the precinct, as there hadn't been time to sort out anything more permanent, and at this time of night she doubted that even he would still be at work.

Her heart began to beat erratically. She was dreading another confrontation. After a minute the answering machine cut in. It seemed she was wrong. Rafe wasn't there. Stacey briefly left a message, hoping it made some sort of sense, assuring Rafe that Max was fine and that she would be back at work on Monday.

Although she had been glad not to

have to speak to Rafe directly and apologise for not having telephoned him earlier, she couldn't help wondering if Rafe was indulging in some overtime at Wade Manor and if Helena Carter was with him.

8

Clutching all the goodies Dolly had pressed on her before she departed Mahon, Stacey grabbed a taxi at Gatwick and headed straight for Wade Manor. The aircraft had spent nearly an hour on the runway before departure while they waited for air traffic clearance, and it was well past midday before Stacey raced into reception to be confronted by a poised Helena seated at the desk.

'Stacey. Good to have you back. What on earth is that?' Her smile turned to a frown.

They both looked at the crushed box of pastries Dolly had thrust into Stacey's hands before boarding, and which she was still clutching as she had clambered out of the taxi.

'I suppose you don't fancy one?' Stacey asked.

'Sorry, I don't think I do,' Helena replied with a charming smile.

'They do look a bit past their best,' Stacey agreed.

'Why don't you put them out for the birds?' Helena suggested. 'I'm sure we've got some nesting blue tits under the eaves. I spotted them the other day.'

Stacey moved the box to one side then looked expectantly at Helena.

'You're in luck, Rafe's out.' Helena read the question hovering on Stacey's lips.

'Thank goodness for that.' Stacey was wearing her freshly laundered sundress and one of Dolly's cardigans. 'I don't fancy being torn off a strip for my unprofessional appearance.'

'I'm sure Rafe wouldn't do that.' Helena looked shocked.

'Do you know if he got my telephone message?'

Helena pulled a face. 'He wasn't in a very good mood about it. I tell you, he was pacing the floor all day Saturday wondering why you hadn't rung. I tried to calm him down. I know what it's like trying to get information out of hospitals and I've never had to do it in Spanish. How did you get on?'

'It's too complicated to explain everything, but Max is fine. He's staying in Menorca for the time being with an old friend. That's about it.'

'As long as your stepfather is well, that's all I need to know really.'

'Thanks for your help,' Stacey began before the ringing of the telephone interrupted them. Helena took the call and Stacey watched her deal with the query with practised ease. She couldn't help wondering again if Helena had been out with Rafe when Stacey had tried to telephone him.

'So in Rafe's absence can you update me?' she asked, dismissing all thoughts of the pair of them together. Whatever Rafe did in his spare time was none of Stacey's business.

'Rafe's drummed up loads of media coverage for the marathon. Shops and restaurants along the route are clamouring for a piece of the action. Most have agreed to make donations to the fund in return for free publicity, and our flyers and leaflets are appearing all over the place. I saw one in a travel agency yesterday next door to a rival health club's advertisement for a spa day. Ours was given much greater prominence and had a little group standing around it discussing the details.'

'That sounds positive.'

'We've got an Olympic medallist to officially start the proceedings and Rafe's trying his best to twist Martin somebody-or-other's arm to sign autographs for a small fee.'

'Who?'

'A freelance reporter. He lives locally. We thought he might do a piece on us too. It's promising to be quite an event.'

'I'm sorry I landed you in it. How have you been coping?' Stacey asked.

'Rafe's put me on the payroll I'm going to be here every day from half nine until half two.'

'Then it's official?'

'I think Rafe felt he might have been asking you to do too much,' Helena said in a faint voice, taking in the expression on Stacey's face. 'I don't mind really. You might have your hands full if your stepfather isn't well?' She looked at Stacey as if seeking her approval. 'Of course, if you'd rather I wasn't here . . . ' she began.

Stacey shook her head. 'We do need a good receptionist and it makes sense to have someone who appears to know the business, although it would have been nice to have been consulted first about your appointment.'

'The weekend was hectic. I hope you don't mind, but I brought my girls in because I don't like leaving them at home alone. They had a lovely time.'

'Your girls?'

'I've got two daughters. Antonia — Toni — is nine and Serena's ten. They've got sponsorship forms for the children's route and they've been busy signing up the workmen. They're quite the little saleswomen. Of course, they get their charm from their mother.' Helena giggled.

'I didn't realise you were married.' Stacey looked at Helena's ringless fingers.

A faint flush worked its way up her pale skin. 'Robert lives in Wales with his second wife. They run a bed and breakfast place so he can't get down here often to visit the girls. They go up whenever they can, mostly during the school holidays.'

'Well, is there anything for me to do?' Stacey changed the subject.

'There's loads. We've got a huge batch of new membership applications. The workmen insist the renovations will be finished on schedule. I've been discussing health and beauty with Rafe and he's interviewing someone tomorrow. She is very experienced and has been looking for a permanent position.'

Stacey swallowed down her silly disappointment over not being involved in the latest developments. She had no right to expect the world to stand still because of disruption to her personal life.

'I'd best be going.' Helena glanced up at the clock. 'School run.' She grabbed her car keys. 'There's a list of telephone messages on the desk, and if you'd like to run through the paper-work?'

'Off you go,' Stacey replied. 'See you tomorrow. By the way,' she couldn't resist asking, 'will you be joining me on my early morning jog?'

Helena's reply was a mocking laugh. 'Me?' she queried.

'Why not?'

'I'll leave it to you. You've made such a good job of delivering the leaflets. We had a deputation of bikers here yesterday all thrusting forms into my face. I tell you, I was a bit scared when they roared into the car park on their huge machines. In the end they turned out to be perfect gentlemen, generous to a fault. Must go. Bye.' Helena ran down the steps. Stacey couldn't help noticing how lithe and fit she seemed. It was no wonder Rafe had signed her up. She was the image Wade Manor liked to portray.

'We're off too.' One of the workmen poked his head round the door that led to the renovated changing rooms. 'Here you are.' He advanced into the reception area on tiptoe. 'Sorry, don't want to leave a muddy mess, but my wife was most insistent I give these to you personally.'

'What are they?'

'More forms. She's manageress of the bakery. Says the biker lads have been coming in en masse to register. You're their new pin-up girl. Respect,' he grinned, depositing more completed sponsorship forms on the desk. 'Everything all right with your dad? Hope you don't mind my asking, but we've all been worried about him.'

'He's fine now, thank you,' Stacey replied. The workman's words created a feeling of warmth in her stomach. It was nice to know people cared.

'Give him our best next time you speak to him.'

'I will.'

'Better go. Rafe doesn't like overalls in reception.' With a wink, he disappeared back into the changing rooms.

The cubbyhole behind reception was pokey and Stacey could smell Helena's perfume. It was a light, fresh aroma and helped to ease the gentle ache at the back of her eyes. Glad to have a few quiet moments now everyone had left, Stacey took the chance to read through the telephone messages and update herself on the latest plans.

There were signed schedules for the treatment room work and another one for the pool. An architect had submitted drawings for a paved terrace area where people would be able to relax with cooling drinks. As Stacey studied them, a shadow fell across the plans. Rafe was standing by the desk, looking at her.

She could read nothing from the

expression on his face; but, mindful of what Helena had said about him not being best pleased about her lack of communication, Stacey cleared her throat carefully before talking. 'As you can see, I'm back. My flight landed at lunchtime and I got here as soon as I could. Helena's been keeping me posted on all that's been going on. I'm sorry I'm inappropriately dressed. I'll change as soon as I can.'

'Max?' Rafe clipped back at her.

'Good afternoon to you too,' she retorted.

The expression on his face didn't change. 'Don't you realise Helena and I have been worried about you? We rang you back after you left that message but all we got was a Spanish maid who didn't appear to understand English. I'm not even sure we rang the right number. We tried the hospital but they said Max wasn't there and they wouldn't give us any further details. How ill is he?'

Stacey frowned. Until now she had

accepted her stepfather's explanation that the reason he had left his cruise was due to a bout of food poisoning, but having had a chance to think things through she wasn't so sure. Any cruise doctor worth his salt would be able to deal with a simple case of an upset stomach.

'Ben was trying to get in touch with you as well,' Rafe went on. 'We were both half out of our minds.'

'That wasn't my fault.'

'How could you be so thoughtless, leaving us without a word?'

Stacey slipped off the stool. When dealing with Rafe she decided it was better to do so standing up. She straightened her sundress and looked him directly in the eye.

'There are three men in my life.' She spoke slowly and carefully. It was important not to lose her dignity, and what she had to say could possibly lead to a loss of composure. 'As far as I can see you're all unreasonable, self-centred, demanding and totally impossible.' Rafe opened his mouth to speak but Stacey forestalled him. 'It's quite all right for Ben to disappear without a word to anyone as to where he's gone. It's fine if Max also falls ill, then disappears somewhere in deepest Menorca leaving a trail of garbled messages behind him, but when I try to find out exactly what's happened to everyone I'm at fault for not issuing hourly updates. How do you think I felt when the only person I could rely on to help me was the cruise ship's agent? It's hardly surprising that telephoning you slipped to the bottom of my list. And as for Ben, the less said about his behaviour the better.'

'I realise things haven't been easy,' Rafe tried to interrupt, but Stacey was on a roll.

'For your information, Max is in great shape. He's lodging with a widowed lady friend, sunning himself by the pool and indulging in long lazy lunches at exclusive waterside restaurants. Ben's fine, too, in case you were wondering. He's got a new lady friend and they're joining forces and hoping Max will fund the painting workshop they want to set up. He also seemed to think I was lax in not informing him what was going on. The only sane person in the scenario was Dolly. I don't know what I would have done if it hadn't been for her.'

Rafe blinked, then leaned in towards Stacey. 'We're not talking cloned sheep here, are we?' he asked in a confidential voice. His face was so close to Stacey's she could see a fine line of stubble on his chin. She blinked, remembering she hadn't thanked him for the upgrade on her flight ticket.

'I beg your pardon?' Her voice came out as a funny sort of tremble.

'Who is Dolly?' he asked.

'She's a friend of Max's and he's going to stay with her. Do you have to stand so close?'

His arm brushed hers as he stepped backwards. 'At the risk of sounding picky, it was you who invaded my body

115

space when you leapt off that stool.' Stacey opened her mouth to protest as Rafe's eyes took in the discarded box of pastries still on the desk.

He flipped back the lid. 'Are these up for grabs? I missed out on lunch.'

'So did I.' Stacey grabbed at another. She licked at the jam as it oozed through her fingers.

'Want to go halves on the last one?' Rafe asked.

Moments later all that remained of Dolly's parting gift was a flat box full of sticky crumbs.

'I was going to feed them to the birds.' Stacey's stomach rumbled its appreciation of the snack.

'They can get their own,' Rafe replied.

'I thought,' Stacey began as she swallowed a crumb that had become lodged in her throat.

'What?'

'You didn't approve of jammy, creamy buns.'

'I don't, and I shall expect you to put

in some jogging overtime first thing tomorrow morning. That is, if you don't oversleep.'

'Why don't you join me?' she invited Rafe. 'I asked Helena but she turned me down.'

'As I will too. I've got an interview to conduct with a potential new beauty therapist.'

'We'd best get on then,' Stacey snapped at him.

Picking up the empty cardboard box, she thrust it into the recycling bin. When she turned back to give further vent to her feelings, Rafe was gone.

9

'Only a week to go.'

Rafe and Stacey were sitting opposite each other at the kitchen table. They had been forced to decamp to Stopes Cottage for the day while the electricians carried out all the necessary tests on the new systems installed at Wade Manor.

'I would never have believed our biker friends would have been so enthusiastic.' Stacey looked at her schedule of jobs done. There was a satisfying amount of ticks on the sheet. 'They've arranged a mobile catering van and marshals along the route. They've bought gallons of water in little bottles to hand out to everyone at designated points and,' she added, 'they've got a tame weatherman to give us a plug on his evening slot when he's doing his forecast the night before the run.'

'What exactly did you do to them outside the bakery?' Rafe enquired. 'I never did get the full details.'

'That's because you were busy chauffeuring Helena around the countryside.'

The moment she spoke, Stacey felt a wash of shame work its way up her neck.

'Helena's not had an easy time of it,' Rafe replied.

'It can't be easy bringing up two girls on your own,' Stacey acknowledged.

'There's more to it than that,' Rafe said in a quiet voice, and yet again Stacey wondered about the true nature of his and Helena's relationship. She often came across them having hurried discussions which were curtailed the moment she entered the room. Stacey had telephoned Rafe at his flat one evening and been surprised when a child had answered the call.

'Mummy's doing some business with Mr Stocker,' she explained.

'Mummy?' Stacey had been trying to

119

gather her scattered wits after first wondering if she had dialled a wrong number.

'Mrs Carter — Helena,' the child added helpfully, then whispered, 'I'm Serena. My sister Toni's asleep on the sofa and I don't want to wake her.'

Stacey had been reluctant to leave a message with Serena and, saying it wasn't important, had rung off. The next morning when she had spoken to Rafe there had been no mention of his previous night's activities.

'You do like her, don't you?' Rafe asked. 'Helena?'

'Yes,' Stacey admitted. She found Helena easy to work with and prepared to turn her hand to any of the daily emergencies as they arose. 'Do you know, I caught her unblocking a drain in the shower room the other day? When I said she didn't have to do that, she told me it was a skill she obtained when she was an airhostess. Apparently life in the galley can be a bit fraught and unless you learn these things early on you won't make the grade.'

'So I've heard,' Rafe replied. 'What do you suggest we do about these?' he changed the subject, indicating the mountain of membership applications for Wade Manor. 'There are too many to go through them all today.'

'I could draft an acknowledgement letter?' Stacey suggested. 'We don't want interest to wane once the marathon has been run.'

They both put out a hand towards the forms and the tips of their fingers touched. With a brief murmured apology, Stacey glanced at the first application. The warmth of Rafe's skin against hers was an unsettling experience.

'I don't believe I've thanked you properly,' Rafe spoke, stalling Stacey.

'For what?' she asked in genuine confusion.

'Did you know Max and my father were once business partners?'

'He did mention it to me,' Stacey admitted.

'Did he mention anything else to you?' There was a wary look in Rafe's eyes.

'He said your father went to Australia when he left the business.' Stacey chose her words carefully.

Rafe nodded. 'I grew up in Perth, Western Australia. Max got in touch when my father died. I told him I was thinking of returning to this country and Max explained about the family business and was I interested in being a part of it? He explained about you and Ben and from what he said I gained the impression that you were a pair of spoilt, overindulged children.'

'I'm twenty-five and Ben's twenty-two,' Stacey reacted. 'That hardly makes us children.'

'All the same, you had many advantages with Max for a father.'

'I suppose you'd already made up your mind about us before we'd even met?'

'You've got to admit it didn't look good when you couldn't even arrive on time for your father's birthday lunch.'

'I've explained about all that,' Stacey brushed aside his comments, 'and despite what you think, life wasn't always an easy ride.' She gestured around the room. 'You can see for yourself that Stopes Cottage isn't exactly the last word in luxury. All Max's capital went into the business and many was the night my mother and I licked envelopes, in the days before everyone was online and the written word was the main source of communication.'

Stacey smiled at the memory of the cosy evenings when they would gather around the log fire and set to with wet sponges for the stamps for the envelopes. The cottage had echoed to the sound of much happy laughter as stamps got stuck in strange places and that was why Stacey loved it so much. For all its lack of luxury, Stopes Cottage was a family home.

'I can't imagine Ben licking envelopes,' Rafe said.

'He was usually away at school,' Stacey replied. 'He came back at weekends but he boarded during the week.'

'And you didn't?'

'I went to the local school.'

Rafe raised an eyebrow. 'Didn't you resent that?'

'What do you mean?' It was Stacey's turn to look surprised.

'Ben had a private education, you didn't.'

'I liked my school and I certainly didn't want to leave when Max and my mother married. Anyway, aren't we wandering off the point? You thought I was a spoilt brat.'

'You did have a private allowance. Not many people enjoy that privilege.'

'Max only gave me a private allowance after I left school. He said it was to make up for all the years of pocket money I'd missed.' Stacey glared at Rafe. She decided there was no need to tell him that she had virtually run the household after her mother had died.

124

Max had paid all the bills but there had been no money to spare.

'Of course,' Rafe agreed. 'It was misguided of me to pre-judge you and I want to say how much I appreciate all you've done. It can't have been easy jogging around Normanswood and the surrounding area every morning, but I've had nothing but positive feedback from the residents.'

'If it's any consolation, although it probably wasn't your intention, I enjoyed it,' Stacey admitted. 'Everyone was so friendly and I had very few doors shut in my face, so your misguided perception of me has had more evidence against it.'

'Did no one tell you it's bad form to crow?' Rafe said, a teasing note to his voice.

'Probably, but then what would I know about things like that? I was too busy licking envelopes to learn about the finer points of life.'

The atmosphere between them relaxed into one of easy familiarity.

Lord and Lady were stretched out in front of the Aga, exhausted by their early morning jog. Stacey didn't take them with her every day, but this morning she had and their sleek presence had proved another attraction. Wilcox was curled up between them and they made a picture of cosy domesticity.

'Do you fancy trying out one of our sponsors' restaurants one evening?' Rafe asked.

'For a meal?' The application form Stacey was reading fell from her fingers.

'I wasn't suggesting we do the dishes. We've lots of places to choose from. The office has been inundated with menus from all the local eateries keen to get in on the action.'

'What about Helena?' Stacey asked.

'Helena?' Rafe frowned.

'Will she mind?'

'I shouldn't think so. We can ask her along if you like, but I thought it might be nice for the two of us to get together without the constant interruptions of the telephone or workmen.'

Stacey blinked. It had been a long time since she had been in a relation-ship, and one thing she knew for certain was that she didn't want to get involved with Rafe. Trying to convince herself she was reading too much into his invitation, she agreed dinner might be a good idea.

'After the race?' Rafe suggested.

The sound of footsteps on the gravel pathway drew Stacey's attention away from Rafe.

'Ben?' she turned to the slender figure silhouetted in the doorway. 'What are you doing here?'

'Hardly the warmest of greetings,' he complained with a sulky look.

Stacey leapt to her feet and, throwing her arms around him, gave him a kiss.

'Steady on,' he protested, returning her hug.

'Why didn't you let me know you were coming?'

'I did. A workman took the call and said he'd pass my message on to you.

I've been waiting for you to pick me up from the station for an hour. When it was obvious you weren't coming I took a taxi.'

'Sorry,' Rafe apologised. 'We're working from home today.'

Ben slumped into the room and threw down his holdall. 'Any lunch on the go? I'm starving.'

'I'll leave you to it.' Rafe stood up and cleared the table of paperwork.

'Did I break something up?' Ben asked.

'No, we're about finished here anyway. I'm sure you two need to catch up. Nice to see you, Ben.' He nodded in his direction. 'See you in the morning, Stacey.'

From the expression on Rafe's face, Stacey suspected that despite his greeting he was not best pleased to see Ben. Stacey too was mildly annoyed that her stepbrother seemed to think she was still available at his every beck and call to rustle up a meal or, as she suspected, eyeing his bulging holdall, to do his laundry.

'Beans on toast?' she asked, looking around for a tin opener.

'Can't you do anything more adventurous than that?' he complained.

'Not at short notice.'

Despite his lack of enthusiasm, Ben cleared his plate, then raided the fruit bowl for a banana. 'Now, what gives?' He sat down at the table and watched Stacey do the washing up.

'Where do you want me to start?' she asked.

'Dad and this Dolly female might be a good place.'

'Is that why you're here?'

'Partly. Fancy a coffee?'

'Only if you put the kettle on.' Stacey was up to her arms in soapy water and had no intention of breaking off from her task.

'Slave driver,' Ben grumbled before throwing her the smile that nearly always got him his own way. 'Where're the supplies?'

'Milk's in the fridge where it has been for the last sixteen years or so.'

Ben began banging cupboard doors in an attempt to get her attention, but Stacey had already turned back to the sink.

'I take it you'd never heard of Dolly and Harvey Travers either?'

'Nope.' Ben flicked the kettle switch. 'And I'm not sure I like the sound of this Menorca business.'

'It really is nothing to do with us.' Stacey finished washing the last plate and dried her hands.

'I happen to think it is. In my experience women of her sort are only after one thing.'

'Women of what sort?'

'Gold diggers.'

'Hold on a minute.' Stacey's raised voice woke the animals dozing by the cooker. They looked at her in mild interest before settling down again. 'You've never met Dolly, so how can you make such a suggestion?'

'I don't have to meet her to know what she's like.'

'She's a very stylish, kind, attractive

woman, and at the risk of sounding indelicate I'm sure she has enough money to cover her needs. She lives in a comfortable villa. She has lots of friends and a vibrant social life.'

'It didn't take her long to latch on to Dad.'

'He latched on to her.'

'You sound as though you approve of the arrangement.'

'I don't disapprove. They are good company for each other. Would you prefer Max to join you in France?'

'What do you mean?' A look of unease crossed Ben's face.

'He's adamant that he's not going cruising again. The doctors prescribed rest in a sunny climate. Where better to convalesce than in Provence? You're always going on about the wonderful climate and the scenery.'

'That's another thing.' Ben skirted around the issue. 'What exactly is wrong with Dad?'

'I think it was nothing more than a case of overindulgence on rich food. He had a stomach upset and chest pains but the tests revealed nothing wrong.'

Ben began to raid the biscuit tin. 'I'm still not happy about it.'

'Then give Max a ring. I'm sure he'd be delighted to hear from you.'

'I might just do that this evening.' He yawned and stretched. 'Is my bed made up?' he asked. 'I've been on the go for hours.'

'Do you intend staying long?' Stacey asked with a sinking heart. Ben created work and right now she had more than enough to do to fill her day.

'I thought I'd give this marathon a try. I've been reading your leaflets all over the place. One turned up in our village.'

'You?' Stacey could hardly believe her ears. 'Participate in a marathon?'

Ben gave a shamefaced grin. 'Only as a spectator.'

'That's more like it.'

'Actually, what I had in mind was painting a picture.'

'Of what?'

'I don't know really. The route? Wade Manor? A Provençal scene personally signed by the artist? Do you think it would make a good raffle prize?'

'I think it's a marvellous idea,' Stacey enthused. 'Don't tell me you thought it up by yourself.'

'That's another thing.' Ben cleared his throat.

'Yes?' Stacey prepared herself for the worst. Ben wouldn't have come home at the drop of a hat without a very good reason. She should have realised that earlier.

'I'm thinking of getting married.'

10

Stacey could hear the crowd cheering before she turned the final corner. She slackened off her pace.

'Thought you were super fit.' Her friend Emily blew a kiss as Stacey sailed by in nifty blue shorts and a T-shirt emblazoned with the Wade Manor logo.

'I am.' Stacey returned her wave.

'Don't believe you. You just want to fall behind the rugby club delegation and look at all those manly legs in shorts, don't you?'

'Would I do such a thing?'

'Yes,' Emily replied with a saucy smile. 'Bye.'

Stacey, hands on her hips, grinned, then leaning forward took some time out to let the rest of the field pass her by. To her surprise, she had been in the lead from the moment Monica Datchett had cut the ribbon to signal the start of the race. Admittedly, many of the entrants were encumbered by their novelty costumes, and the children kept stopping to wave to their grandparents or inspect the flowers on the wayside. All the same, she had been surprised how easy the course had been.

The weather had pulled out all the stops and a glorious May sun shone out of a cloudless blue sky. Stacey hadn't expected to get a wink of sleep the previous night, but she had slept like a log. To ensure there was no chance of her oversleeping, she had set two alarms and her clock radio to full volume. All had burst into life at the appointed hour, rousing Stacey from the deepest of sleeps and setting Lord and Lady off in a frantic scrabble for the back door to escape the noise. After her shower, the smell of burnt toast lured her downstairs, where she found Ben preparing breakfast.

'I've walked Lord and Lady, so there's no need to worry about them.

Help yourself.' He indicated his culinary efforts. 'It's a bit charred, but with a dollop of honey it'll settle the stomach. Goodness knows when we'll get anything proper to eat.'

Ever since his shock announcement about his wedding plans, Ben had done his best to enter the spirit of the charity mini-marathon. He had painted posts along the route, designed multi-coloured markers to ensure no one got lost, helped tie the ribbons to keep back the onlookers, and generally made himself useful in a variety of different ways. During the week leading up to the big event, Stacey didn't know what she would have done without him, especially as Rafe had taken to disappearing at odd moments without any explanation. Helena, too, had seemed distracted, often leaving Stacey to answer the constant ringing of the telephone.

There hadn't been much time to discuss Ben's marital affairs, but after a quick telephone call to Max in

Menorca, Stacey had overheard Ben telling his father about someone called Yvette. Discreetly closing the kitchen door, Stacey had let them enjoy the rest of their conversation in peace.

After forcing down a couple of slices of Ben's blackened toast, Stacey had arrived early at the race starting point to find it already seething with activity.

'Mind the cables, love,' a cameraman called over. 'Don't want any accidents. That young lady said it was all right for us to set up here.' He indicated Helena who, stunning as always, was wearing pink shorts to accompany her Wade Manor top. After kissing Stacey on the cheek and posing prettily for a magazine picture, she had taken it upon herself to look after the celebrity guests. Of Rafe there had been no sign.

'Haven't seen him,' Helena informed her, before being called away for yet another photo shoot. 'I expect he's around somewhere.'

Martin Biggs, the freelance reporter,

was proving a great attraction and had a queue of hopeful autograph-hunters clutching their programmes for him to sign. Stacey waved over to him and received a cheery smile in return.

'Lots more donations for the pot,' he said as he pointed to a huge glass jar by his side. It was already half full.

'Should make a good article.' Stacey decided there was no harm in reminding him he had promised to do a piece on the big day.

'I hadn't forgotten. Honestly,' he confided to a young mother in the queue, 'she's such a slave driver.'

'You should have seen her take our lot on,' one of the leather-clad bikers winked as he walked by. He was clutching a little boy's hand.

'We're going to start halfway down,' the child confided. 'Aren't we, Daddy?'

'Don't give our secrets away,' he said. 'They don't all have to know I'm not as fit as I look.'

'Half the route's better than none,' Stacey laughed back at him. 'You'd better get a move on. We're due to start any minute.'

'See what I mean?' There was the chink of more coins going in the glass jar as Martin Biggs finished signing another programme. 'She doesn't let up.'

'Like the outfit?' After breakfast Ben, too, had dressed for the occasion and Stacey burst out laughing at the sight of him wearing an artist's smock and a black floppy hat, in the style of the Flemish masters. He was carrying a fake palette and brushes and causing much hilarity by pretending to throw a strop when one of the young mothers refused to pose for him.

'Really, I cannot work with amateurs,' he said in a shrill voice before mincing off.

Stacey began to suspect she had walked through the looking-glass after indulging in a long conversation with a chicken, a juggler, a pantomime dame and a science fiction character. She didn't have the faintest idea who he was but he seemed to know all about her, as did most of the entrants.

More bikers were out in force, helping parents locate children who had wandered off in all the excitement, and dogs who had slipped their leads.

'All animals to be tethered please,' a voice bellowed through a megaphone. 'This is a fun day and we don't want any disasters. Now is everyone ready? Miss Datchett, please will you do the honours?'

Sporting a huge pair of fake scissors and looking incredibly glamorous in a red dress and high heels, the medal-winning sprinter held up the scissors for the benefit of the camera crews before snipping at the bow. With a roar and much excited laughter, the contestants surged forward.

That had been over half an hour ago, and Stacey had still not spotted Rafe. Helena, too, seemed to have disappeared.

Deciding at least one representative of Wade Manor should complete the course to do the honours at the finishing line, Stacey caught up with the last of the stragglers. A loud roar and much good-natured bantering greeted her arrival as she raced past the post.

'Here she is. Let's have a cheer please for the last but not least, the lovely Stacey Oliver,' the commentator boomed down the microphone.

A brass band struck up a rousing chorus of congratulations that was almost drowned out by the whistles and rattles of the more boisterous element of the spectators, fuelled — Stacey suspected — by enthusiastic rugby club supporters.

'How do you feel now the race is over?' A microphone was thrust under her nose.

Brilliant,' she managed to gasp before a cry went up, 'Look, it's St Joseph's.'

All heads turned back to the course to where a happy trail of children — some in wheelchairs pushed by carers, others trotting happily by their side, followed by a squad of helpers

— began their descent down the hill towards the crowds who were cheering them on. The noise was deafening as one by one they crossed the line.

A little girl hopped towards Stacey. 'You're the lady who delivered the posters, aren't you? Did you see? I ran all the way. My legs didn't give out.'

Sally Good, with her bespectacled daughter Melanie, rushed forward. 'We made it, too. We weren't sure we would, but Melanie's had the op,' her mother whispered. 'Everything's fine. The doctors are so pleased with her progress that they gave her special permission to be here today. Actually,' Sally glanced over her shoulder, 'I expect I shouldn't tell you this but there's a consultant or two somewhere about the place.'

A portly-looking man was busy sipping some water provided by one of the bikers. 'Can't do this too often,' he joked. 'My waistline, not to mention my dignity, aren't up to it.'

'Mr Stocker helped me,' another little boy announced importantly, and he beamed at Stacey through the gap in his front teeth.

Stacey's eyes crashed into Rafe's, who was hovering on the edge of the excited group. 'How on earth did you manage it?' Stacey asked, caught up in the swarm of activity.

'It was touch and go at times,' he murmured, 'but the children so wanted to be a part of the big day. We didn't want them to be disappointed. All present and correct, I think. Helena?'

She appeared at Rafe's side. The smile she threw him was enough to convince Stacey that her earlier suspicions about their relationship had been correct. No woman could look so adoringly at a man unless she was in love with him.

'We owe you so much,' she said in a breathy voice.

'Nonsense,' Rafe replied. 'It was a team effort. Wasn't it, girls?'

It was then Stacey noticed two children hovering behind Helena. They were wearing summer dresses and huge straw sunhats and Stacey could instantly see their resemblance to their mother.

'I'm Serena,' the slightly taller one introduced herself. She had a protective arm around the younger girl. 'This is Antonia, my sister. We call her Toni.'

'I'm very tired,' Toni said in a quiet little voice.

Helena immediately turned her attention away from Rafe as one of the nurses produced a chair for the pale-faced child. She sank into it with a grateful sigh. Stacey could see the dark circles under her eyes and turned a questioning glance towards Rafe.

'Toni's a resident of St Joseph's,' he explained, 'and our special guest today.'

'I don't think we'll be able to stay for the prize-giving,' Helena said. 'Toni's exhausted.'

Rafe put an arm around her waist. 'Can I see you home?'

'No, you stay here. We've got plenty of help. Thanks, Stacey.' Helena threw her a grateful look. 'You've done so much to make the day a success. I want you to know how much St Joseph's appreciates all your hard work.'

Feeling ashamed of her earlier suspicions of Helena's motives for wanting to help, Stacey waved to the two girls, who were now being shepherded through the crowds towards a backup vehicle.

'Over here,' Ben bellowed from the winner's podium. 'You're missing all the action. Come on, Stace. Bring Rafe with you, if you must,' he joked. 'Personally I prefer Miss Datchett's company, but I suppose today of all days one must make sacrifices.'

Ben's banter was going down well with the crowd and they roared approval at all his dreadful jokes. Stacey allowed him to take centre stage. When it came to this sort of thing he was a natural, and her own emotions were too entangled to enter into lighthearted badinage with the organisers.

'Now, the moment you have all been waiting for: the raffle. First prize, as you all are no doubt aware, is by famous local artist Ben Wade. That's me, for those of you still in the dark as to who on earth I am. Miss Datchett, if you'd be so kind as to pick a ticket out of the drum?'

'The winner is,' she paused, then announced with a girlish giggle, 'number forty-nine, Rafe Stocker.'

A chorus of boos and 'it's been fixed' greeted the announcement.

Rafe stepped forward from the back of the stage and, taking the microphone from Ben, announced, 'Unfortunately my efforts to snaffle this very valuable work of art appear to have been rumbled. I fear I have no other choice but to ask the delectable Miss Datchett to repeat the performance.'

'That's more like it,' a voice called from the crowd.

'Come on, Monica, do your stuff,' another joined in.

This time the winner was a respectable middle-aged man who turned out to be the mayor. He promised to hang his prize in the town hall for all to see.

'Fame at last,' Ben announced. 'Today the town hall, tomorrow the Louvre.'

The bank manager presented a token cardboard cheque to the management of St Joseph's, with the promise of a fund top-up to be added to the total when the final figures were in. One of the children then presented Monica Datchett with a huge bouquet of flowers, which she accepted with a pretty speech of thanks.

'I think this day has been more rewarding than when I won my medal. And if you all want to do it again next year, then I'll do my best to be available.' Her words were met with a mixture of cheers and groans.

'Before I draw things to a close,' Ben had again grabbed the microphone again, 'I have one more duty to perform.'

An expectant hush fell on the crowd.

'Some of you may not know this, but I am Stacey Oliver's brother. My father married her mother when we were both quite young. At first I was appalled at the idea of having a big sister interfering with my life and I'd like to put on record she can be extremely bossy at times.' A bout of laughter greeted this remark. 'However,' Ben went on, 'on the whole, although she has her faults, I couldn't ask for a nicer big sister.' Stacey could feel her face colouring up as all eyes turned in her direction. Rafe squeezed her hand.

'I know how you hate being the centre of attention, but I think there's no stopping Ben now.'

'I hope he isn't going to be too embarrassing and start mentioning our childhood spats.'

'I can see by the look on my sister's face that I'm going to have to cut things short.' Ben glanced in her direction. 'I think she's scared I'm going to tell you about the time she locked me in the shed then lost the key. I seem to remember she went to bed hungry that night.' Another howl of laughter greeted this story. 'Moving swiftly on, before she takes a pot shot at me with a catapult — and that wouldn't be a first, I can assure you — I have been advised by the organisers that we've raised more than four times our expectations, and that's before we've had a proper chance to total up all the donations.' This announcement was met with a roar of approval. 'I couldn't let such an achievement pass without a gesture of appreciation to Stacey.'

Stacey groaned and wondered what was coming next as the rugby club fans began to chant and stamp their feet.

'So, Stacey, if you'd like to step up onto the stage.'

'Go on.' Rafe nudged her in the ribs, catching Stacey off balance. She toppled into a local dignitary sporting a huge official chain, and with a murmur of apology disentangled herself before making her way to the podium, doing her best to control her shaking legs.

'Rafe too,' Ben urged and gestured

him forward. There was another round of cheering as he stood by Stacey's side.

'Now with grateful thanks from the organisers, the entrants and of course St Joseph's,' Ben announced as one of the children appeared with another bouquet of flowers, 'we would like to present you with this token of our appreciation.'

The little girl performed a very pretty curtsey as she handed over the flowers, and Ben finished with, 'Good on you, Stacey.'

'Thank you, darling,' Stacey smiled at the child. 'They're beautiful.'

'Look this way, please.' Stacey blinked into the lens of a photographer's camera. 'Mr Stocker, if we could have a publicity shot of you and Miss Oliver together?'

'Certainly.' Rafe obliged, standing by Stacey's side.

'Would you stand closer together please?'

The little girl cuddled into Stacey's legs and Rafe put his arm around Stacey's waist, making it impossible for her to move.

'Right now, how about a kiss?'

'Of course,' Rafe replied. 'Anything for publicity.' Before Stacey realised his intention, his lips were on hers. In the background she heard a roar from the crowd and the sound of a battery of cameras as the photographers took their photo.

11

Rafe's kiss aroused sensations in Stacey she had never experienced before. Her fingertips tingled and she lost control of her legs. As she arched her back and steadied herself against Rafe's body, she could feel the twin beat of his heart against hers. She struggled to break free from his embrace but without success. His hand was clamped firmly around the back of her spine and with the little girl's arms still tucked around her legs, short of being seriously undignified there was nothing she could do to extricate herself.

As they finally drew apart a loud burst of applause greeted Rafe's gesture along with good-natured cries of, 'You'll have to marry her now.'

All around them flash bulbs exploded as the photographers got the shots they were looking for.

Aware of her heightened colour, Stacey had been forced to keep smiling and pretend her pulse rate was perfectly normal. 'My poor blooms are squashed,' she joked, indicating her flowers, some of which had been crushed against her chest by Rafe's embrace.

His light brown eyes were lit with mischief as he retaliated with, 'Can't have you losing your blossom, can we?' He tweaked a stray petal out of her hair, all the while still looking at her. For a moment neither spoke. It was as if they were alone on a desert island, not standing on a podium, the centre of intense media attention and speculation.

'Have I got pollen on my nose?' Stacey eventually demanded, wishing what felt like a thousand pairs of eyes weren't fixed on her.

'No,' Rafe admitted, his trademark slightly crooked smile turning his mouth up at the corner. 'I'm actually plucking up the courage to ask you something.'

'I've never known you to suffer from shyness before,' Stacey challenged back at him.

'There's quite a bit about me you don't know,' he retaliated.

'What is it you want to ask me?' Stacey was having trouble keeping her voice casual.

'Will you come out to dinner with me tonight? As a celebration?'

'I can't,' Stacey replied firmly, her head still reeling from the intensity of his kiss and ignoring the traitorous inner voice in her head telling her to accept.

'Why not?'

'I'm busy,' she improvised.

The faint flicker of attraction she had felt for Rafe when he kissed her withered and died as she came to her senses and recognised it for the moment's madness it was. How could she even think about accepting his invitation? Helena was at home nursing her sick child. Rafe should be by her side, offering comfort and support, not arranging dinner dates with another female.

'Doing what?' Rafe persisted.

'I've got mountains of paperwork.'

'Which will keep.'

'Ben's home too. We usually have dinner together to, you know,' Stacey injected a light hearted note into her voice, 'discuss the day, that sort of thing.'

Rafe glanced over her shoulder. 'I think you'll find from the intensity of his conversation with Miss Datchett that your stepbrother has other plans for this evening.'

Stacey followed the direction of his gaze and swallowed hard. Were all men the same? Ben was engaged to Yvette. Rafe and Helena were an item, yet neither of the men appeared averse to inviting another woman out for the evening.

'If you must know, I'm tired and I'd rather spend the evening on my own.' Stacey saw no reason to spare Rafe's feelings and decided to give up all pretence of being polite.

'Another time perhaps?' he suggested.

'Rafe?' a voice called his name before she could give vent to her feelings.

'What?' he snapped.

'You're needed. Something to do with a last-minute donation?'

'Can't you deal with it?' A look of irritation crossed Rafe's face.

'It's a large sum of money,' a volunteer murmured in his ear, 'and I don't really want to take the responsibility for all that cash. Sorry, Stacey. Am I interrupting something?'

'Not at all. If you'll excuse me, Rafe. I really should see about some refreshment for the helpers.' It wasn't a good excuse, but the best she could come up with at short notice, and she made a swift escape before Rafe could think of a further reason to detain her.

Now the main business of the day was over, people were beginning to drift away.

'Stace!' Ben waved across to her.

'What plans have you got for this evening?'

'I could grill some salmon steaks?'

Ben cleared his throat. 'Actually,' he began, 'can we put the salmon on hold?' He moved in closer. 'I've been talking to Monica Datchett,' he began.

'And you prefer her company to mine?' Stacy didn't bother to disguise her annoyance. 'What about Yvette?'

Ben raised his eyebrows. 'She would understand.'

Stacey sighed. 'As you wish. What time do you think you'll be back?'

'Stace,' Ben wheedled, 'she's a useful contact. Monica knows loads of people. She's going to give me some names and addresses. This could be my big chance. I won't be late, I promise, but best not wait up for me.'

Assuring Ben she had no intention of doing any such thing, she kissed him on the cheek before watching him drive off in Monica's car.

Stacey, with time on her hands for the first time in a long while, wondered what to do with the rest of her evening. She didn't want to go home to an empty cottage, but she certainly wasn't going to accept Rafe's offer of dinner. Now the race was over, she was injected with a feeling of anticlimax. Already the buzz was beginning to die down. The cameras had packed up and gone, and technicians were busy dismantling the public address system.

She helped the litter monitors tidy up, then took down the bunting draped above the finishing line. By the time she had spoken to nearly everyone on site, munched on a burger and drank numerous cups of tea, it was growing noticeably cooler and the light was beginning to fade from the day. Calling out her goodbyes and again thanking everyone for their help, she could think of no further reason to linger at the site.

She began to trek back to the designated parking area in the company of the last remaining volunteers. After saying goodbye, she began to fumble in her body belt for her car keys. In the encroaching twilight it wasn't easy to see what she was doing. All around her she could hear cars starting up and leaving the car park. Luckily there was no sign of Rafe. She wondered briefly if he'd found someone to fill her place for the evening.

Careful not to drop her keys in the long grass where she would have difficulty finding them in the half-light, she turned the lock to the driver's door. The clock on the dashboard revealed it was later than she had thought. Grateful that her next-door neighbour had promised to see to Lord and Lady during the afternoon, Stacey started up, engaged first gear and began her drive home.

The evening air was soft after the heat of the day and Stacey wound down the window. A smell of honeysuckle invaded the car interior and she took a deep breath of the sweet scent. In the distance she heard the hoot of on a barn owl. She stifled a yawn behind the back of her hand. Her eyelids felt heavy.

It wasn't far to Stopes Cottage, but Stacey knew it was important to drive carefully and to pay attention to her speed. The night air through the open window refreshed her jaded senses, but she didn't want her concentration to lapse or to drift over the speed limit.

She blinked, then frowned. Her eyes were tired but she was certain she could see a lone light blinking at her out of the darkness like a beacon guiding her home. It grew stronger as she drove towards it. Was she more tired than was immediately apparent?

A few moments later she knew she wasn't mistaken. She was driving along the lane, parallel to the road leading up to Wade Manor, and the light she could see was coming from Rafe's office. Swiftly turning her steering wheel, she double backed the way she had come, fighting down her fears that someone had broken in. It wouldn't have been difficult to work out that the centre would be deserted all day.

She eased up on the accelerator. She

couldn't call for back up help. Her mobile was in her handbag and she had left them both in Stopes Cottage. There hadn't been room to carry anything personal during the day, apart from her keys and a small bit of change in her body belt. She debated whether or not to turn around again, but whoever was in the club might hear the sound of her tyres or see the reflection of her lights, besides which the back lane was notoriously narrow and she stood the very real risk of winding up in a ditch.

Instantly dismissing the thought that it could perhaps be one of the workmen on overtime, Stacey decided the only thing to do was to confront the intruder. She had the advantage of surprise and if things turned nasty, at least the telephones were connected on site.

Holding her breath, she carried on inching forward, keeping the engine noise as low as she dared without stalling the car. Strange shapes loomed at her from out of the darkness and night noises emanated from the under-growth. There was a loud screech before something landed in the stream with a loud plop. In the background the steeple of the church tower stood starkly etched against the purple sky. Stacey had never noticed before how isolated Wade Manor was, but with the light fading from the day it took on the appearance of a deserted Gothic mansion.

The light was shining out from a window that was too high up for her to identify the housebreaker, but from the shadows playing on the ceiling she could now see she wasn't mistaken in her suspicions. There was definitely an intruder on the premises. Parking as close to the building as she dared, Stacey turned off the engine, then as quietly as she could she opened the driver's door and slipped out of the car. Holding her breath, she moved towards the front of the building and headed towards the main doors. The light was coming from the first floor, so the intruder would appear to know his or her way around the centre. The lock hadn't been forced and neither had the alarms gone off. Stacey frowned. The only people who knew the code to disconnect the alarms were herself, Helena and Rafe.

She took a few moments out in reception to steady her breath. Above her she could hear the muffled sound of movement. She had to act now.

Looking around for a suitable weapon, she grabbed up a Nordic walking pole. She hesitated at the foot of the stairs before beginning her ascent. The corridor was in darkness, save for the slit of light coming from a crack underneath the door to Rafe's office. Seizing her moment, Stacey plunged forward.

'Caught you!' she shouted, lunging through the door and waving her walking stick in the air.

The sight that met her eyes caused her to lose her hold on the stick. It fell from her fingers and landed with a dull clank onto the floor.

The intruder turned towards her in shock. Only it wasn't an intruder. It was Rafe Stocker, and he was standing in the middle of the room busily stashing cash into a large briefcase. In the far corner of the room the safe was wide open, and from where Stacey was standing she could see it was empty.

12

'Like father, like son,' Stacey yelled, taking in the scene before her eyes.

In one careful movement Rafe put the briefcase down on the desk, then looking her straight in the eye, demanded in a cold clear voice, 'Exactly what do you mean by that remark?'

'Isn't it obvious? Max told me all about your father and why they fell out.'

'Did Max also tell you that his suspicions about my father were unfounded?'

Too late, Stacey remembered that was exactly what Max had told her.

'That was the reason why my father moved to Australia. He couldn't stand the shame. When Max realised he had been wrong he tried to rectify the situation but by then it was too late.'

'I spoke without thinking,' Stacey admitted in a hollow voice, but Rafe

165

didn't appear to be listening.

'Max and my father never met again. After my father died, Max wanted to make up for his past suspicions and that was why he offered me the position here.' Rafe paused. 'It would seem you don't share his trust in my integrity.'

Stacey looked around the room. In his shock, Rafe had dropped several wads of notes onto the floor.

'If you're as innocent as you say you are, then what are you doing here?' she demanded.

'Cashing up,' Rafe replied. 'That last-minute donation was extremely generous and I wanted to lock it away as soon as possible. As you turned down my invitation for the evening, I decided there was no time like the present to get on with it.'

Stacey's eyes strayed towards the briefcase.

'I wasn't thinking of making a break for it with the proceeds of the mini-marathon, if that's what was on your mind.'

'It wasn't, actually, but you were putting the money into a briefcase.'

'Correction, I was taking it out.' Rafe picked it up. 'The briefcase belongs to the donor. I asked if I could borrow it and he agreed. I intend to return it to him in the morning. Due to the generosity of various sponsors throughout the day, I found myself in the position of having more cash on my person than I would have liked. I decided that after I had made a running total I would put it all in the safe ready to take to the bank on Monday morning. That's why the safe is empty.'

Stacey blinked hard, uncomfortably aware that she owed Rafe the biggest apology of her life, but not sure how to go about it. She was in an embarrassing situation of her own making and she didn't know how to get out of it. Not for the first time she had jumped to the wrong conclusion about him, and not only had she maligned his good name, but she had also maligned that of his father.

'Rafe,' she began, 'I spoke out of shock and the surprise of finding you here. It was wrong of me to suggest that you or your father have ever been up to anything underhanded.'

Rafe acknowledged her apology with a brief nod of his head, then said, 'You haven't told me what you are doing here.'

'I was driving home and I saw the light on,' she began to explain. 'I didn't think anyone would be working here this late today of all days, so I decided to investigate.'

'Did you intend to use this on me?' Rafe stooped down to pick up the ski pole.

'I don't know what I intended,' Stacey admitted.

'Don't you realise how foolish such an action would have been?' he demanded. 'If I had been a criminal bent on mischief you might have been seriously injured.'

'There was nothing else I could do.'

'There were plenty of choices. Why

didn't you call for backup for a start?'

'I haven't got my mobile on me and I thought whoever was in the office would overhear if I made a call from the switchboard.'

'So you decided to tackle the intruder single-handed,' Rafe's eyes worked their way up her jogging pants to her flimsy top, 'wearing minimal protection?'

'I'm sorry,' she apologised, 'for everything — for being foolish, for being rude, for saying what I said about you and your father.' She swayed. Rafe was by her side in an instant.

'Sit down for goodness sake. You look exhausted.' He yanked an office chair out from behind the desk and with little ceremony pushed her down onto it, then thrust her head between her knees. Stacey, her head swimming, took several large gasps of air, then coughed as Rafe thumped her between the shoulder blades.

'Have you eaten?' he demanded as she struggled to an upright position.

'I had a burger, I think.' Stacey frowned as his blurred image came back into focus.

Rafe opened a desk drawer. 'Here.' He thrust a chocolate bar at her. 'Want to share it with me?' Without waiting for a response, he unwrapped it and cracked it in half. 'Eat,' he ordered her.

The melted caramel, nuts and nougat, and rich milk chocolate melted in Stacey's mouth. It had been weeks since she had eaten anything this sweet and she was unable to prevent a sigh of satisfaction escaping her lips. Leaning against the hard back of her chair she closed her eyes, missing the expression on Rafe's face as she savoured every morsel of their shared treat.

'Better?' his voice interrupted her pleasure.

'Mm,' Stacey mumbled, opening her eyes and wiping her mouth, aware there were still flakes of chocolate on her lips. 'That was absolutely delicious.'

'There's one bit left.' Rafe looked down at the desk. 'Toss you for it?'

'You lost.' Her spirits restored, Stacey snatched out with her hand and popped the chocolate into her mouth, laughing at the look of outraged surprise on Rafe's face. 'You can't make me spit it out, that would be unladylike.'

'So is cheating,' Rafe protested.

'In this world nice guys come last.'

'So now you think I'm a nice guy?'

'I didn't say that,' Stacey hedged.

'Right then, as a forfeit you can help me add up this lot and put it all back in the safe, which as you will recall I was trying to do before you attempted to club seven bells out of me. In fact,' he picked up the pole, 'I think I'd better put this in a safe place.' He lodged it against a wall. 'In case you get any more urges that you can't control.'

'Where did all this money come from?' Stacey demanded, glad to have a distraction between them.

'Helena raised a lot of it.' Rafe noted down some figures on a pad of paper.

'How?'

'She's the administrator of the St

Joseph's charity. She's very hands-on and there's a lot involved. What with taking on the job here and looking after her two daughters, she's had more than enough to do, but she still found the time to think up ways of raising more money. That's why we've been working late. I've been helping her. Figures aren't her strong point. A new assistant has been appointed and he'll be starting next week, so that will ease her load. He's actually an old family friend of hers and I think they've got a bit of a thing going between them. I hope so. Helena deserves some good luck. How much have you got there?'

Stacey read out some figures and Rafe duly noted them down. Her head was whirling again. She had been so wrong about him from every aspect. He wasn't involved personally with Helena; neither was he a latter-day crook. She didn't know what she could have been thinking of to accuse him the way she did. She burned with shame at the memory and hoped Rafe wouldn't take the incident further.

'There, all done.' Rafe swung shut the door to the safe about half an hour later and straightened up. 'Glad we got that sorted. Actually,' he cleared his throat, 'I've another favour to ask you. Don't worry, it isn't another invitation out to dinner. I've eaten.' He dropped the empty chocolate wrapper into the wastepaper bin. 'Can you give me a lift? I was going to call up a taxi.'

'I don't call half a chocolate bar dinner,' Stacey replied.

'It's all I'm going to get this evening.'

Stacey took a deep breath. 'Ben turned down my offer of a grilled salmon steak. Would you be interested?'

'I think I would,' Rafe admitted.

'Do you always park your car in the road?' Rafe demanded as Stacey positioned it outside the hairdressers in what passed for the main street of Normanswood.

'Max has a lock-up garage I sometimes use, but it's a five-minute walk away and it's down a horrible back lane. I don't really like using it after dark. You can't get a car down Lavender Lane, so in answer to your question, yes. Ready?'

She locked the car. Rafe lessened his pace to match that of Stacey's as they ambled up the incline towards Stopes Cottage. Stacey swung open the gate just as a shaft of light was cast across the tiny patch of lawn. Ben stood framed in the doorway to the cottage.

'Where've you been?' he demanded.

'We were working late,' Rafe explained before Stacey could reply.

'I've been trying to get hold you for hours. I've been ringing round everywhere I could think of but no one knew where you were.'

'Has something happened to Max?' Stacey asked as they congregated in the confined space of the vestibule.

'He's fine,' Ben added quickly. 'No need to worry, but he's booked a video call later. Says he wants to talk to us.'

'What about?'

'I have absolutely no idea, but that's

why I've spent the best part of my evening trying to track you down.'

'What are you doing back here so early anyway? I thought you were going out to dinner with Monica Datchett.'

'So did I, but her boyfriend turned up and made it very obvious that three was a crowd,' Ben said, a dissatisfied look on his face, 'so I came home. Didn't you mention something about salmon steaks?'

'Which I've now promised to Rafe.'

'Look,' Rafe intervened between the pair of them, 'It's time I was getting home. I'll call that taxi.'

'No need,' Stacey insisted. 'There's more than enough for all of us, but I'll need some help.'

With the two men busy laying the table, then taking Lord and Lady out for a much-needed walk, Stacey busied herself in the kitchen. Soon the steaks were sizzling under the grill and some fresh new potatoes were simmering on the hob. Adding some mint from the herb garden, she gave them a quick stir.

'That smells good.' Ben and the dogs came back into the kitchen, followed by Wilcox the cat who, only after a dignified stretch that totally blocked the doorway, deigned to let Rafe in. For a few moments chaos ensued in the kitchen until Ben managed to sort everyone out.

'We should have eaten on our laps,' he complained as Stacey made him sit at the table.

'We have a guest,' she reminded her stepbrother sharply.

Ben waved a forked potato at Rafe. 'Brilliant day, wasn't it? Do you know how much we raised?'

'Only a rough estimate,' Rafe replied, 'and there's more to come in.'

The conversation flowed easily throughout the meal. Ben volunteered to do the dishes after they'd finished eating, while Rafe brewed some coffee, leaving Stacey free to rush upstairs for a quick shower and the chance to change into some fresh clothes.

'Look at the time.' Ben settled on the sofa next to Stacey and leaning forward, switched on the laptop. Moments later the screen was filled with a tanned and relaxed-looking Max, a smiling Dolly by his side.

'Hello, everyone,' he greeted them. Dolly smiled and waved at the camera. 'For those of you who haven't been introduced, this is Dolly Travers.'

'Nice to meet you all.'

'My son Ben is seated next to Stacey,' Max said, 'and behind them is Rafe Stocker.'

'We've been reading all about you and the mini-marathon in the local English language newspaper.' Dolly smiled at Rafe. 'You're quite a star.'

'Yes,' Max took up the story, 'when the editor realised my connection with Wade Manor they sent a reporter over to interview me. I'll email a copy over when it's printed.' He held up a batch of envelopes. 'I've even received some donations for St Joseph's. Good stuff. How did everything go?'

'It was a roaring success.' Stacey smiled at Max.

'I'm sorry I missed it, but well done you.'

'It was Rafe's idea,' Stacey felt duty-bound to point out.

'We all did our bit.' Ben's voice was beginning to verge on grumpy. He didn't like not being the centre of attention.

'How are you now, Max?' Stacey asked, anxious to avoid confrontation between father and son.

'Never felt better. That's the reason I arranged this video conference. I'm glad you're all there so that I can break the news to everyone at the same time.'

'News?' Ben echoed.

'Dolly and I have decided to get married and you're all invited to the ceremony.'

13

The Gothic church at the top of the hill was a perfect setting for the wedding. A lazy spring breeze took the heat out of the sun, making it a pleasant afternoon. Down in the harbour small boats bobbed on the jewel-bright water.

A flower-bedecked white painted carriage pulled by two horses, their bridles also bedecked with spring blossom, delivered Dolly to the church a respectable quarter of an hour late for the ceremony, by which time Ben had his hands full calming Max down.

'She's not coming.' His father twisted round in the front pew and looked over his shoulder for the fifth time in as many minutes.

'She'll be here,' Ben assured him, his mouth set in a grim line.

Their news had come as a bolt out of the blue, and while Stacey was pleased for Max and Dolly, she could see Ben wasn't so sure.

'They've only known each other a matter of weeks,' he protested.

'It's a lot longer than that,' she insisted. 'They go back years.'

'You know what I mean.' His close-set blue eyes deepened in colour, an indication that if Stacey didn't handle things carefully she could be on the receiving end of some sharp words.

'Dolly explained that her sensibilities about living in the same villa with Max and not being married to him were making her feel uncomfortable.'

'So she says.'

'Can't you be pleased for them?' she pleaded.

'The situation strikes me as being very convenient for Dolly.'

'Perhaps it is. They're both widowed and lonely and they get on well together. What could be more natural than their getting married?'

'We know little about her.'

'As far as I know she hasn't robbed a

bank or broken the law in any other way.'

'You know what I mean. She'll be Max's next of kin and we all know where that could lead.'

Stacey bit her lip. It was her private opinion that over the years Ben had wheedled more than his due out of his father and if his marriage to Dolly stemmed the flow, it might be no bad thing. At the age of twenty-two, Stacey couldn't help feeling it was time Ben stood on his own feet and stopped relying on his father to finance his lifestyle choices.

'Will Yvette be coming to the wedding?' she asked.

'I haven't told her yet,' Ben mumbled. 'We'll see.'

'I look forward to meeting her.' Stacey smiled brightly, hoping she had defused any potential flare-ups.

Ben had reluctantly been persuaded by his father to take on the role of best man, with Stacey as Dolly's chief attendant. Dolly, dressed in an ivory silk dress and bolero jacket and clutching a small bouquet of violets, was given away by an old friend, an elderly gentleman who had been her bridge partner for many years. Now standing in front of the small altar, she and Max exchanged vows and were pronounced man and wife. The look of love Max bestowed on Dolly as he placed the ring on her finger convinced Stacey that despite Ben's fears, they were doing the right thing.

'Are you married?' a small local flower girl asked as Stacey tried to control her fit of the fidgets.

'No,' Stacey whispered in reply.

'Why not? You're very pretty.'

Blushing, Stacey hushed the child and did her best to ignore indulgent Spanish smiles cast in her direction. Stacey was glad Rafe had decided not to accompany her to Menorca, although he had been invited to the wedding.

'It's a family affair,' he explained.

'You'd be very welcome,' Max had

insisted over a second video link when he had sounded out Ben and Stacey regarding their duties during the service.

'I know, Max, and I'm grateful to have been included on the guest list, but I feel Stacey and I shouldn't both be away from work at the same time.'

'Have it your own way,' Max said, accepting Rafe's decision. 'Dolly has issued an open invitation to visit whenever you like, so can we expect you here some time during the summer?'

'I'll look forward to it,' Rafe assured him.

Deciding a break from Rafe was a good idea, Stacey had been relieved about Rafe's decision to miss the ceremony. The situation between them was still tense, even though he appeared to have accepted her apology over the accusations she had flung at him the night she had discovered him standing by the open empty safe.

The success of the mini-marathon

was still being talked about and donations continued to pour in from people who had only recently heard of their cause.

'I don't like leaving you with all this work,' Stacey voiced her concerns to Helena, 'even though Rafe will be here.'

The receptionist had returned to her duties but now worked reduced hours. Antonia had been undergoing new treatment to stabilise her condition, but had developed an allergy to some of the methods used, which meant more of Helena's time was taken up with home nursing duties. With the health club membership list growing by the day, it was obvious extra help would be needed.

'You have to go,' Helena insisted. 'Charlie can help out here. My new assistant.' She blushed when Stacey threw her a querying look. 'Charlie's been helping out at St Joseph's with the admin work. I've spoken to Rafe about him and he's happy with the arrangement. We've put him on the bank of staff. You know someone we can call in to help at short notice?'

Stacey bit back her annoyance. Even though she now knew their relationship was purely professional, decisions were still being taken between Helena and Rafe without her knowledge. 'If you're sure?' she ventured hesitantly, not wanting to make an issue of the situation.

'I'm sure,' Helena assured her. 'But there is something you can do for me,' she began. 'Could you bring two fans back for the girls, black lace? They were so excited when I told them about the wedding, I sort of promised them a gift. It wouldn't be too much trouble, would it?'

'Two black lace fans it is,' Stacey replied. 'That's if I ever get out there.' She eyed the mountain of application forms that was threatening to topple over at any moment.

By dint of working late every night for a week and catching up on telephone calls in bed, Stacey managed to clear her desk before she flew out to the island a few days before the ceremony. Dolly had been delighted to see her, and together they had shopped for the last minute bits and pieces her new stepmother-to-be considered essential for her big day.

'It's not a very grand affair,' she explained. 'Some locals, a few friends, club acquaintances. We've both been through it before, and frankly at our time of life, neither of us wanted a big show.' Dolly squeezed Stacey's fingers. 'You don't mind, darling, do you?'

'About the wedding?'

'I'm not trying to replace Penelope, Max's first wife, or your mother in Max's affections. Without his two previous wives I wouldn't have inherited his wonderful children, would I? It's a little late in the day for me to have a family of my own, so a ready-made one is such a bonus.'

'I'm very pleased for you.' Stacey hugged Dolly. 'I must admit I was worried when Max said he was retiring for health reasons, but with you by his side, I know he's in safe hands.'

'Bless you,' Dolly whispered, 'I do love the old so-and-so very much, even if he can be a bit obstinate at times — and when he digs his heels in there's no changing his mind, but there you have it. By the way, I absolutely promise not to act the wicked stepmother.'

'I've never had one before. A stepmother,' Stacey admitted. 'It'll be a new experience for us both.'

'What about Ben?' A small frown wrinkled Dolly's brow. 'I sense he isn't quite so enthralled by events.'

'I wouldn't try to pull the wool over your eyes, Dolly,' Stacey confessed after a short pause.

'I should hope not,' Dolly bridled. 'I've always been one to speak my mind and I don't want any secrets between us either.'

'Ben feels that everything has been a bit rushed.'

'It has,' Dolly admitted, 'but Max started suggesting we go away on holiday together and well, call me old-fashioned, but I felt it would be more appropriate if we were married. At my age it seemed silly to refer to a man in his sixties as my boyfriend.' Dolly giggled like a young girl. 'You should have seen Max's face when I proposed.'

'I would have given anything to be there.' Stacey joined in her laughter.

'I told Max I would go on holiday with him, but only as his wife. Then I asked him if he'd do me the very great honour of being my husband. I didn't go down on one knee, but it was like it is in the films. I have to admit I held my breath so long my chest hurt. In the end I had to prompt him for answer.'

'Thank goodness he said yes.'

'My thoughts entirely.' Dolly held out her hands. 'And now here we are, me a blushing bride and Max a dashing groom. Who would have thought it? You never know what's around the corner, do you?'

'No indeed.'

'Did I tell you we finally caught up with the captain of Max's cruise ship? We got his luggage back. It was in a bit of a sorry state because it had been crammed in a storeroom. As compensation we've been offered a complimentary trip to Cyprus, courtesy of the company, so right after the ceremony we're off. Max says he won't mind being on board because this time I'll be there to fend off anyone being a nuisance. Now,' Dolly's butterfly mind had already moved on to the next topic, 'didn't you say something about black lace fans? I know just the place. Follow me.'

The wedding reception was held at the country club adjacent to the golf course, which meant all the guests had to do was walk the short distance from the church to where a marquee had been erected for their exclusive use.

Despite Stacey's fears, Ben fulfilled his best man tasks by delivering a surprisingly kind and witty speech, during which he revealed a few amusing anecdotes about his father's past behaviour before welcoming Dolly to her new family and asking her if she was aware of what she was taking on. Upon Dolly's assurance that she did, he asked everyone to toast the happy couple before again asking the guests to raise their glasses for a second toast, this one to the chief bridesmaid.

'She can be a bit of a tyrant at times,' Ben revealed, 'especially on a Sunday morning when I do like a lie-in and she has other ideas.'

A sea of laughter greeted this remark.

'On a purely personal note, she was there for me at a very vulnerable time of my life, something I'll never forget.' He picked up his glass and added in a soft voice, 'To Stacey.'

Seated at the top table, Stacey flushed and was relieved when at a bidden signal from Ben the musicians began to play, diverting everyone's attention away from her. This speech-making habit of Ben's was getting a little embarrassing.

After a simple meal of freshly caught red mullet and an exotic fruit salad, some children wearing traditional dress had entertained them afterwards, performing dances and singing local songs.

'That was quite some speech,' Stacey said to Ben later when they managed to have a quiet moment together.

'I meant every word of it,' he replied. 'Let's hope Dolly and Max look out for each other too.'

'They will,' Stacey assured him, glad he now appeared to have accepted that their marriage was a good thing. 'I'm sorry Yvette couldn't be here,' Stacey said.

'She wanted to come, but like with Rafe and you things are busy and only one of us can be away. This painting workshop plan of ours seems to be taking off. Hopefully you'll meet her in the summer if I can persuade her to take a holiday.'

'And your wedding plans?'

'Definitely put on hold after this development,' Ben said with a trace of his earlier doubt in his voice. 'Dad's not mean — far from it — but with a new wife he's not going to want to splash money around unnecessarily.'

'The minibus is ready,' a voice announced from the tent flap.

'Where are we going now?' Ben demanded.

'Didn't you know? Dolly and Max are off on a cruise to Cyprus. We're all going to wave them goodbye.'

Grumbling that no one told him anything, Ben went in search of his jacket.

Down on the quayside the vessel was waiting for the happy party. As Dolly and Max were played aboard by the ship's band, Dolly turned to Stacey; and before she realised her new stepmother's intention, Dolly threw Stacey the bouquet of wild violets she had been clutching throughout the journey down to the harbour. Amidst cheers and happy smiles, Stacey had no option but to catch it. With a wicked smile, Dolly blew her a kiss before she and Max boarded the ship. The wedding party continued on the quayside until an hour or so later when, with streamers flowing from the deck and the sound of the band striking up more romantic music, the ship finally eased out of the harbour.

'It's just you and me now, isn't it?' Ben smiled down at her.

Stacey didn't answer. Not wanting Ben to see her emotions, she was busy pretending she had something in her eye.

14

'Good morning,' Rafe greeted Stacey as she arrived for work on Monday morning. 'How did the wedding go?'

'I know I'm late,' Stacey gasped. 'We were held up by air traffic control again last night. It's a busy time of year. We didn't land until midnight. Then I couldn't get a taxi home for another hour, and before you ask I haven't been jogging this morning. I forgot to set my alarm and I overslept.' She glared at him defiantly, her eyes flashing as if ready for action.

Rafe's lips twitched. 'Which is rather where we came in, isn't it?' he enquired.

Stacey began to feel rather foolish standing at the bottom of the reception steps looking up at him. 'I wanted you to know the position, that's all,' she replied.

'Well I'm glad you've got everything off your chest,' Rafe continued in a calm voice, 'and to set your mind at rest. I wasn't actually thinking of scouring the countryside for you. You could have taken more time off if you'd wanted to. You must have loads of hours owing.'

Stacey gave a shamefaced smile. 'You know your trouble, Rafe?'

'What?' he demanded with a frown.

'You bring out the worst in me,' she admitted.

'I'm sorry to hear that,' he replied gravely. 'I'll try not to in future. Now the wedding?'

'The sun shone all day. It was a lovely ceremony, very low-key, exactly as the newlyweds both wanted, and everything went off without a hitch. Ben's best man speech was well received and I managed to dissuade my restless co-bridal attendant from deadheading her flowers in the church and scattering petals up the aisle.'

'Sounds like you did well.'

'At the end of the afternoon everyone went down to the harbour and waved the happy couple off on their honeymoon cruise.'

'A cruise? I thought with Max it was never again.' Rafe raised his eyebrows in surprise.

'The company offered him and Dolly complimentary places on a trip to Cyprus and Dolly leapt at the chance. She said she'd always wanted to visit Aphrodite's island, so Max gave in.'

'Good for Dolly. It sounds like she's already taking charge.' Rafe opened one of the double doors for Stacey to pass through. 'By the way, your tan suits you.'

'There wasn't much time for sitting around in the sunshine.' Unused to receiving compliments from Rafe, Stacey did her best not to lose her footing. 'Dolly doesn't take prisoners when it comes to shopping.'

'So I can see. What's in the bag?' Rafe eyed her purchases with interest.

'Lace fans for Toni and Serena, a

shawl for Helena and olives for you.'

The last purchase had been made at Dolly's urging. She insisted Rafe shouldn't be left out just because he was a man and Stacey had fallen in with her wishes, hoping she'd made the right choice. From the expression on Rafe's face she suspected that Dolly had got it right yet again.

'You didn't have to do that but thank you.' Rafe inspected the jar of stuffed Manzanilla olives. 'I shall look forward to enjoying them.'

'Where's Helena?' Stacey glanced over Rafe's shoulder.

'She'll be in later. Toni's got a hospital appointment.'

'How is her daughter?' Stacey asked as she put the presents down on Helena's desk.

'Getting better now they've identified her allergy. Charlie is looking after them, driving Helena around and that sort of thing. He's been helping out here too, filling in membership cards, updating the database and making himself generally useful.'

Stacey stared at the newly refurbished reception area. One or two members were drifting around in fluffy white shower robes displaying the new Wade Manor logo a friend of Helena's had designed for them. There was a loud splash from the swimming pool and the sound of laughter as someone blew a whistle.

'Aquarobics,' Rafe explained.

'The work is finished?' Stacey couldn't keep the surprise out of her voice.

'Fully up and running. Membership numbers have trebled and Wade Manor is now on the map. We've had a lot of enquiries from St Joseph's, would you believe. I thought about offering a special children's package. What do you think?'

'It's a marvellous idea,' Stacey enthused. 'We could do something for the carers as well, a special discount perhaps?'

'That's what I had in mind.'

'Mr Stocker?'

'Coming. I'll catch up with you later.' Rafe strolled off to talk to one of the instructors from the gym.

The remainder of the morning passed in a blur as Stacey answered numerous telephone enquiries, dealt with a flood in the shower room caused by a foreign object lodged in the outlet pipe, and tried to tally up the latest charity donations still trickling in from the proceeds of the marathon. Even though she'd only had a few hours of sleep, there wasn't time to feel tired.

'Sorry to disturb you,' a voice interrupted her calculations.

'Emily?' Stacey looked up at her friend. 'What are you doing here?'

'I'm the new beauty therapist.' She held up a vast leather bag. 'The tools of my trade,' she explained. 'Didn't Helena tell you?' she prompted as Stacey still looked at her in confusion. 'She arranged for me to start today.'

'I haven't seen her.'

'Of course, I was forgetting — it's

your first day back isn't it?' Emily leaned forward. 'I hear Max has got married again? Great news. I suppose he won't be coming back to work now, will he?'

'I don't suppose he will,' Stacey agreed. 'He seems to be settled in Menorca. The climate suits him and Dolly, his new wife, is a social lady. Even if he wanted to I don't think he'd have time to return to work.'

'Where does that leave you and Rafe?' Emily lowered her voice in a confidential tone, her blue eyes alight with intrigue.

'For the moment nothing changes,' Stacey replied, keen to get Emily off the subject of Rafe. Although she hadn't seen much of her friend lately, Emily wasn't exactly the most discreet person in the world, and if she suspected anything of a personal nature between Stacey and Rafe the consequences would be all over town in no time.

'Are you and he,' Emily paused as she chose the right word, 'involved?'

'Of course.' Stacey watched with satisfaction as the light of intrigue died in Emily's eyes when she added, 'We are business colleagues.'

'Talking of business,' she said, 'isn't he the business?'

'Rafe is also your new boss,' Stacey reminded her friend sternly, 'so I would suggest you get down to work, bearing in mind you're late on duty and it's your first day.'

'All right.' Emily's sunny smile didn't slip as she picked up her bag. 'Show me where to go.'

Although it would appear another decision had been made without her input, Stacey had to admit having a beauty therapist on the staff was a good idea. Emily was well qualified and loved her work.

Helena arrived mid-afternoon looking a little less composed than usual. She seemed to have made an attempt to secure her ash blonde hair in a scrunchie, but several strands had worked loose and her topknot looked in danger of complete collapse. She kissed Stacey on the cheek. 'I am so glad to have you back,' she enthused after Stacey had given her an account of the weekend. 'One more day of Rafe and I'd have been handing in my notice.'

'You can't mean that.' Stacey could hardly believe what she was hearing.

'I do,' she said grimly. 'He's been driving everyone mad. The man believes in getting his pound of flesh out of the workers.'

Stacey smiled. 'Have you only now worked that one out?'

'I told him I wasn't prepared to put in as many hours as you and it was about time he recognised how hard you work.'

'That must have gone down well,' Stacey laughed. 'Anyway, these are for you.'

Helena's eyes lighted on the presents. She took a peek at the delicate lace fans. 'They are lovely. Toni was only asking me yesterday if I thought you'd remember.' Helena draped the pink shawl around her shoulders. 'And this is absolutely perfect. I'll wear it tomorrow night. Charlie is taking us bowling. By the way, he's promised to collect the girls from school for me later, so why don't you go off early? You must be exhausted.'

'Good idea,' a voice interrupted them.

Stacey swung round. She hadn't realised Rafe was standing behind the desk. 'I was actually going to propose we go out to dinner tonight, Stacey, but I didn't know how we were placed for reception cover.'

'There you are then.' Helena smiled. 'Problem solved. Off you go. Have a nice time.'

'Hold on,' Stacey protested.

'What's the matter now?' Rafe demanded.

'I can't go out to dinner with you.'

'Why not?'

'I haven't unpacked.' Stacey knew she was blushing under the scrutiny of two pairs of unbelieving eyes.

'Now you're making excuses.' Helena was the first to speak. 'Who cares if you've got a mile-high pile of dirty laundry? It'll wait. Believe me, no one ever said they wished they'd spent more time doing their washing when asked what they regretted about their life.'

'My thoughts exactly,' Rafe agreed with Helena.

'That new brasserie's offered us a special deal.' Helena began searching through some leaflets. 'Here we are, two for the price of one on all main courses. Now what girl could refuse an offer like that?'

'We could put it down to overtime,' Rafe coaxed, 'if your conscience is tweaking you. I've tried to visit the establishments involved in the marathon to thank them for all they did for us, but this one's slipped through the net.'

'Stacey will be ready at eight o'clock.' Helena's firm voice carried across reception.

'If you're not interested, I'm available.' Emily, who happened to be passing through, grinned across at them.

Stacey bit down a gesture of annoyance. Now Emily had got wind of things, there was no point in turning down Rafe's invitation to dinner. Her friend would put the word round that they were an item anyway.

'I'll see you later, then,' she replied.

'For goodness sake,' Helena hissed as Rafe went back to the office, 'try to look happy about it. Half the females who frequent this establishment would give anything to be in your shoes. Now off you go.'

Wallowing in a warm bath, Stacey let the lemon-scented steam relieve the stresses of the day. The bath oil had been a wedding gift from Dolly, who'd had it especially made up at a little pharmacist on the island.

'They do the most incredible body rubs,' she had explained as she booked both of them into the spa for a full massage and facial.

'Dolly, you can't,' Stacey had protested when she'd been presented with the miniscule bottle of eye-wateringly expensive oil.

'Of course I can. I'm having some too. I've got to the age when my beauty routine needs all the help nature can give, and what's wrong with spoiling my new daughter?' she demanded.

Stacey squeezed her sponge and let warm water trickle down her arm. She couldn't help noticing how her recent exercise routine had tightened up her muscles. Since Max had taken early retirement, her life had completely changed. With her thoughts drifting along these lines, she leaned back and closed her eyes.

'What?' she shrieked, splashing water all over the floor as she awoke with a jolt to the sound of someone hammering on the front door.

Lord and Lady began barking, prepared to ward off intruders. Wilcox, snoozing on the bathroom shelf and enjoying what remained of the day's warmth, opened a lazy eye and closed it again as if the effort of making a move was all too much for him.

Stacey leapt out of the bath and, grabbing up her shower robe, secured it firmly around her waist; then she twisted another towel around her damp hair. To her horror she realised exactly how efficacious Dolly's bath oil was. She had been asleep for over an hour.

'Stacey?' Rafe was now rattling the letterbox. 'Are you there? Answer the door.'

'Yes, I'm here.' Breathless from having raced down the stairs, Stacey nudged Lady out of the way and checking her appearance in the hall mirror, unlatched the door. She peered at Rafe, who was standing on the doorstep. Lord poked his head through the gap, his nose twitching at the fragrant smells coming from the container of takeaway food Rafe was holding.

'The brasserie's closed on Monday and Tuesday nights,' he confessed with an embarrassed smile.

'Our date's off?' Stacey could not

disguise her relief.

'Certainly not,' Rafe replied. 'Naan bread, chicken curry, fried pepper rice and vegetable samosas are definitely on the menu. I also have a large jar of Manzanilla olives that I thought we could enjoy with an aperitif. I'm, er, glad you didn't bother to get dressed up.' He glanced down at her shower robe.

'I fell asleep in the bath,' Stacey confessed, tugging at the belt of her bathrobe.

'All right if I come in? I could put these into the oven to warm while you dry your hair.'

Stacey backed away from the open door. 'It's that way.' She waved in the general direction of the kitchen. 'I won't be long.'

Slipping into a casual top and her favourite pair of cargo pants, Stacey dealt with her hair, trying to ignore the increasing level of noise downstairs. She hid a smile. Perhaps she ought to have told Rafe that Lord and Lady, after their years of enforced racing diets, now had to be the greediest dogs she had ever known. He would have his work cut out if he could get their supper into the oven in one piece. At the sound of more barking, she glanced out of her bedroom window and saw Rafe romping on the lawn with the dogs. The evening sun slanted on his hair, highlighting the blond streaks that hadn't darkened to mid-brown. Her breath caught in her chest. She could see why Emily thought as she did about him. He was an extremely attractive, eligible bachelor and if that wasn't enough to get the pulses of most of the females at Wade Manor racing, she didn't know what would. Stacey bit her lip in an effort to persuade herself that her own pulse was beating perfectly normally. As if sensing her presence, Rafe glanced up to her window and waved.

'Five minutes?' he called out.

Stacey's stomach reminded her she had eaten very little that day and that it was more than ready for nourishment.

Rafe had done his best with the table, laying place mats and finding matching glasses. Max and Ben had never really gone in for home entertaining and most of the plates at Stopes Cottage were a mismatched collection of various bits and pieces of crockery they had acquired over the years.

'Sit down,' he greeted her. 'I know it's your cottage but I hope you'll allow me to wait on you. You don't mind eating in the kitchen?'

'We nearly always do,' Stacey replied. 'It's the one room in the house that doesn't have a floor that slants.'

'I'm glad you said that,' Rafe replied. 'I sipped some wine before you came down and I began to think I'd overdone it.' He poured her out a glass. 'In honour of the occasion I went Spanish, a bold and fruity red. At least that's what it says on the bottle.'

Soon the table was laden with an assorted selection of Indian dishes and a large bowl of olives. 'Tuck in,' he urged.

'You really should let me do that,' Stacey protested as after their meal Rafe began to fill the sink with warm water.

'Nothing to do,' he insisted. 'The foil containers are already in the landfill and I've rinsed out the glasses and cutlery. There.' He turned around to face her. 'Now what do we do?'

'Shall we go through to the other room?' Stacey stood up, not sure where the rest of the evening was going.

'Good idea. I'll bring the coffee through.'

Choosing some late-evening mood music, Stacey flicked a switch on the player and plumped up the cushions. Her heart was beating a tattoo and she was glad when Lord and Lady provided a distraction by flopping down in front of the log-effect gas fire Stacey had turned on to take the chill off the room.

'I managed to get the last box of chocolate mints from the newsagents before they closed up for the night,' Rafe explained, opening up the box and passing it over. Without waiting for an invitation, he sat down beside her on the sofa and put a casual arm around her shoulder.

Quite how it happened Stacey didn't know, but the next moment Rafe's lips were on hers. He tasted of a mixture of olives and chocolate mints. Her head swirled and she was glad of the support of the cushions behind her back. Eventually Rafe released her, his eyes glittering in the half-light.

'Do you think one of us should answer it?' he enquired in a voice thick with emotion.

It was then Stacey realised the ringing in her ears wasn't from the effect of Rafe's embrace, but the telephone.

'It might be an emergency,' Rafe said.

Stumbling across the room, Stacey picked up the receiver.

'Stace? Hi, it's Ben. Everything OK?'

She cleared her throat. 'Fine. Yes.

How about you?'

'I feel great. The reason I'm calling you so late is because I wanted you to be the first to know. I got married this afternoon.'

15

'We didn't want to steal Dad's thunder,' Ben explained after Stacey had got over the shock and recovered her sense sufficiently to ask why no one from the family had been invited. 'I couldn't mention anything earlier because our plans weren't clear, but that was the reason why Yvette couldn't make the ceremony. She was sorting things out here. There were masses of people to contact and formalities to complete and what with the new art project we are developing she didn't have the time. Anyway, here she is. She'd like a word with you.'

'What? No. Wait a minute. Ben?'

''Allo, Stacey?' A gentle voice enquired.

Stacey stared across the room at Rafe. 'What's happened now?' he mouthed at her.

'It's Ben.'

'I gathered that.'

'Are you there?' the voice down the line enquired.

'Yvette? Yes. Sorry. Congratulations,' Stacey replied. 'What a surprise.'

'Thank you. I regret that we have not yet met, but Ben has told me all about his big sister. I hope we are going to be very great friends.'

'Thank you. I'm sure we will.'

'You will come and visit us when we are settled?'

'I'd love to.'

'Good. I put you back to your brother now?'

Stacey placed her hand over the receiver. 'He's married,' she whispered to Rafe.

'Not another one. There seems to be an epidemic of nuptials in your family.' Rafe paused. 'I hope you're not thinking of catching it?'

Stacey's mouth dried. Her lips still hadn't fully recovered from the intensity of his kiss. If Ben's call hadn't interrupted their embrace, her heartbeat raced at the prospect of what rash promises she might have made.

'Stace? Me again.' Ben laughed.

'What about Max?' Stacey demanded. 'How are you going to let him and Dolly know your news?'

'We'll probably wait until we get back.'

'Where are you going?'

'We're off to Spain to chill out for a few days. Yvette's got some friends outside Seville. We're going to visit them then maybe drive on down to Granada. Yvette's never visited the Alhambra. Neither have I, come to that. Anyway, I promise to keep in touch if I can find an internet café, but don't worry if you don't hear from me for a few days. Who's that I can hear in the background?' he asked.

'It's, er, Rafe,' Stacey admitted.

'Is it indeed? Dinner à deux was it? And there's me thinking you'd be lonely without Dad or me to keep you company. Don't do anything I wouldn't do. Cheers. Gotta go. Bye.'

'I've re-heated the coffee.' Rafe came back into the room. 'You look as though you could do with a cup.'

'Did you get all that?' Stacey asked, warming her hands around the mug Rafe thrust into them.

'The general gist of things, yes. Sorry,' he apologised, 'didn't mean to eavesdrop, only I couldn't really avoid it.'

'I don't know where this leaves us.' Stacey sank against the cushions.

'I don't understand.' Rafe frowned.

'If Ben settles in France — and it looks as though he will — and I'm certain Max will stay in Menorca, that leaves you and me running Wade Manor on our own.'

'Is that a problem?'

'I don't know.'

'We've managed quite well on our own up to now, haven't we?'

'Yes, but Max promised to fund Ben's art for a year. This marriage may change things.'

'Their agreement still has ten months or so to go. There's nothing much we can do about things for the time being. I gather Max doesn't know that he's acquired a daughter-in-law?'

'No.' Stacey stifled a sigh.

Yet again, Ben's actions had put Stacey in an awkward position. It wasn't her place to tell Max that Ben was married, but Rafe was right. He shouldn't be kept in the dark. On the other hand, Stacey wasn't too sure exactly where Max was at this precise moment. Dolly had said something about leaving the cruise ship at Cyprus because she wanted to visit Paphos to see Aphrodite's rock, and it wasn't a trip included in the itinerary.

'Ben's a grown man. He can sort out his own life,' Rafe assured her. 'Now he's got himself a wife, he's going to have to take on more responsibility.'

'That's another thing. What about Yvette?' Stacey demanded.

'What about her?'

'If she's an astute businesswoman,

she may want a share in Wade Manor.'

Rafe finished his coffee. 'One thing's for certain, we can't do anything for the moment.' He glanced at the clock. 'I'd better be on my way. If you want to take a few days off I don't mind.'

'What for?'

'I don't know. To catch up on your laundry perhaps?' Rafe asked with a quirky smile.

'I'll be in as usual tomorrow morning,' Stacey assured him. 'Thank you for dinner.'

'My pleasure.' Rafe hesitated, then with a brief nod he said, 'I can see myself out. Make sure you get a good night's sleep.'

*   *   *

Stacey settled down to a routine of going to work, dealing with the day's problems, then coming home in the evening, walking the dogs and settling down for a quiet night in.

Emily had been agog to hear Stacey's

news and, like Helena, was intrigued to know what Ben's new wife was like. The pressure of work eased now the renovation of Wade Manor was complete, and Stacey began to wonder where she was going with her own life.

There were no more dinner dates with Rafe and it was as if their passionate kiss had never been. Rafe had kissed her twice now, and each time it had been an earth-shattering experience, but Stacey knew they meant nothing to Rafe. If they had, he would have asked her out again, but he hadn't.

Helena's friend Charlie proved to be a delightful man, and Stacey was pleased to see that his relationship with Helena was deepening into something serious.

The girls had been thrilled with their fans and written Stacey pretty letters of thanks, illustrating them with drawings of exotic dancers flashing similar fans as they performed their intricate dance steps.

'I suppose you don't fancy a night out?' Emily enquired at the end of another routine week.

'What exactly do you have in mind?' Stacey asked warily.

Emily's idea of a good night out could often turn into an early morning to bed experience. Stacey wasn't sure she had the stamina any more. She still went jogging as a matter of routine, but early morning starts and late nights didn't really mix well.

'Rafe gave me some vouchers for the brasserie,' Emily explained. 'As I'm between boyfriends at the moment, it seems a shame to let them go to waste. I tried getting Rafe to suggest we go together but I could see I was wasting my time. He ever-so-politely gave me the brush off.' Emily eyed her friend enquiringly. 'It seems you never got there either, to the brasserie?'

'They were closed.'

Emily nodded and to Stacey's relief let the matter drop. 'If you're doing nothing this evening, I'm free, and tomorrow is Saturday, so you can lie in.'

To Stacey's surprise, they had a good time. The brasserie turned out to be a newly converted warehouse not far from Normanswood. Their taxi dropped them in the car park and as they got out, they could hear the strains of dance music coming from inside. The dining area was light and airy and offered a wide range of dishes. When the proprietor found out who Stacey was, he insisted their drinks were on the house.

'The marathon brought in a lot of new business,' he explained, 'exactly what we needed to get this place up and running. Have a good evening.'

The live band played throughout the meal, and afterwards when the dancing began, Stacey and Emily weren't short of partners.

'You look as though you're enjoying yourself,' Emily said as they took a rare moment out to sit down and refresh themselves with some orange juice.

'I am,' Stacey admitted.

'It's been a while since we've been out on the town, hasn't it?'

Stacey nodded. 'There hasn't been much time, what with Max retiring and then the marathon.'

'I think we're getting old,' Emily laughed. 'The sort of nights out we used to have don't appeal to me anymore. This is much more my scene.' The band began to play a slow number. 'Looks like we're up for another dance.'

A man Stacey thought she recognised invited Emily to dance and another hour passed before either of them finally sat down again.

'We ought to think about leaving,' Stacey said, massaging her legs, 'before my feet give out.'

'I've been offered a lift home,' Emily confided, 'and I've wangled you a lift too. We can drop you on the way. Don't look so worried. I know Jack. He runs a building company. He did some work for my mother.'

'I thought I recognised him,' Stacey said.

'Actually, I've had my eye on him for a while. I'm going to try and sign him up for membership of Wade Manor. That way I can accidentally bump into him on purpose. What do you think?'

'I think you're shameful.' Stacey eased her aching feet. 'But a lift home would be very acceptable.'

'I'll get the coats.'

Stopes Cottage was in darkness as Stacey inserted her key. Fumbling for the light switch, she saw she had missed two messages while she had been out. She felt the swish of a tail against her legs as Lady came to greet her.

'Want a quick walk?' she asked, stroking the silky coat.

The night was fresh, and cleared Stacey's head after the warm atmosphere of the brasserie. The two dogs spent several minutes sniffing around the undergrowth, exploring the source of new smells.

'Come on,' Stacey eventually called over to them. 'Time to go home.'

The telephone was ringing again as

she dried their paws in the kitchen. They settled down in their baskets as Stacey went to answer the call.

'There you are,' Dolly said as she lifted the receiver. 'I've been trying to get you all evening. Didn't you get my messages?'

'I've been out, Dolly. I've only this minute got back. Then I had to take the dogs out — Dolly, what is it?' Stacey asked. Dolly sounded as though she had been crying. 'What's the matter?'

There was a long pause. 'I don't know how to tell you this,' she began.

Stacey gripped the receiver, quelling the urge to shout at Dolly.

'Max and I had a lovely honeymoon. We went to Aphrodite's Rock and I swam in the water. Silly, I know, but there's a legend that it makes you beautiful. I didn't take all my clothes off, of course, as you're supposed to, but the water was lovely and warm.'

'Dolly,' Stacey implored, 'you didn't ring me to tell me you'd taken a dip in the sea, did you?'

'No,' Dolly agreed, 'I didn't. We — ' she hesitated, 'we got back late last night. To be honest we were both absolutely shattered. Max said he didn't want to disturb me, as he often gets up in the night to make himself a cup of tea if he can't sleep, so he said he'd sleep in the spare room. I crashed out in the main bedroom and didn't wake up for hours. It was mid-afternoon before I went in search of Max. Fiorella was in the kitchen and she said she hadn't seen him.' Dolly gulped as if she were having trouble breathing. 'When I went to check up on him in the spare room he was still asleep — at least I thought he was. I put my hand out to touch his face and that was when I realised.' Dolly was openly crying now.

'Dolly, no.'

The dogs whined at the sound of Stacey's raised voice. Through her tears she heard Dolly tell her, 'The doctor says it must have been very peaceful.'

16

'There is no mistake, Miss Oliver,' the solicitor informed her. 'I also have here a letter from Mr Wade. It is personal and addressed to you.' He passed it over. 'I trust it will explain everything.'

Hardly bothering to glance at it, Stacey slipped the envelope into her bag. Her fingers were trembling and it nearly slipped out of her hold. The shocked expression on Ben's face was almost more than she could bear. As for Yvette, her new sister-in-law, she had hoped the two of them would be friends but she doubted if that would be possible. Obviously Yvette's loyalties lay with her husband, and now she, too, was looking at Stacey as if she were the manipulator behind this latest development.

Stacey stole a glance at Rafe. He was staring in front of him, betraying no sign or emotion of any kind as the solicitor also passed him a personal letter from Max.

Dolly, who might have been Stacey's only ally, wasn't present. Apart from a token bequest of one of Max's paintings, she hadn't been mentioned in the will at all. This, she had told Stacey before she had flown back to Menorca, had been her wish.

'Max said we ought to draw up new wills before we got married. As my own dear Harvey left me more than adequately provided for, I told Max he wasn't to leave me a penny. I didn't want to be the cause of any family discord. We discussed it in depth and eventually he came round to my point of view,' Dolly had informed Stacey. Her eyes were red rimmed and she was clutching a soggy tissue. 'I've been blessed in many other ways that money could never buy.' She did her best to smile. 'I've had two lovely husbands and although my time with Max was short, I've got fond memories of our time together.' She gave a loud sniff. 'Now, remember, if everything gets too much for you here, you're to fly out to me, any time, open invitation.'

'What do you mean the funeral's taken place?' Ben had demanded when Stacey finally tracked him down.

'Dolly arranged it all. There's to be a memorial service in this country. As most of Max's friends are here, it made sense.'

'Max was my father; surely I should have had a say in his affairs.'

'We tried to contact you, but we had no idea how long you would be on your honeymoon or where you were, so in the end Dolly went ahead with her own plans.'

'I can't help feeling the two of you are trying to cut me out.'

'What on earth do you mean?' Stacey had been appalled by Ben's take on the situation.

'When Dad first fell ill, you flew out to Menorca but you didn't bother to contact me to tell me what was going on, and now this.'

It would do no good telling Ben he was being totally unreasonable. Stacey could only put his behaviour down to intense grief over the loss of his father. 'I'm sure if he'd known about your marriage to Yvette he would have made further provision for you.' Stacey did her best to placate him after the will was read the day following the memorial service, but she knew he wasn't listening. The mulish expression on his face reminded her of his teenage tantrums.

When they had all been asked to meet up at the solicitor's office, Stacey had been as devastated as everyone else to learn that Max had bequeathed her the deeds of Wade Manor with the proviso that she was to be in charge of the day-to-day running of the centre. If it had been a gesture of reparation for all the years he had refused to listen to her feminist views about a woman's place in business, then by his generosity he had created a rift between her and

Ben that might never be healed.

'My father left my stepsister everything?' Ben had repeated in a stunned voice.

The solicitor began to look uncomfortable. 'Not everything, no. You have been left Stopes Cottage and other financial assets.'

'But nothing in the business?'

'That is the case.'

'Is there any way the will can be re-written?' Stacey suggested.

'There is,' the solicitor replied, 'but it's a complicated process and are you sure that's really what you want to do? Go against your stepfather's wishes?'

'If I may be permitted a word?' Rafe interrupted in a quiet voice.

'By all means' The solicitor looked relieved as everyone turned to look at him.

'Max placed his trust in me, and you,' he added, addressing Stacey, 'to turn Wade Manor's fortune around. Something I think we've done. It is now thriving and a focal point of local life.

To shut it down would tear the heart out of the community.'

'I wasn't suggesting shutting it down,' Stacey began.

'That's the only way you'll be able to offer Ben anything meaningful by way of reparation for the terms of Max's will.'

'Right, well, obviously my father knew what he was doing,' Ben butted in. 'I wouldn't want to be held responsible for wrecking the community. I am, however, in serious need of funds. Stopes Cottage will have to be sold.'

'It's our childhood home. You can't be serious,' Stacey gasped.

'And you can't have everything,' Ben retaliated. 'You've got the business and all that goes with it. You're also living rent-free in my property. I'm sorry, Stace, the gravy train stops here. I'm giving you notice to vacate the premises as soon as possible before I put it on the market.'

There had been no further chance to

talk to Ben in private. He and Yvette had returned to France on the next available shuttle. Stacey's only consolation had been a swift hug from Yvette as they made their goodbyes.

'I will try to talk to Ben for you,' she whispered, 'but now without his father's generous allowance, we may have to re-think our plans for the art project. It is a great pity.' Her words were far from the assurance Stacey had been seeking.

'Ben didn't appreciate when he was well off,' Emily said later as she dropped by Stopes Cottage to see how things had gone with the solicitor. 'He's never done a day's proper work in his life and now he's been forced to stand on his own two feet, he's blaming you for something you haven't done.'

'Max was his father. I was only his stepdaughter. It doesn't seem fair.'

'That's as maybe, but you worked your socks off for Wade Manor. You were out jogging at dawn. You delivered brochures. You unblocked the plumbing. If Rafe hadn't stopped you, you'd probably have rebuilt the swimming pool. What did Ben do while all this was going on? I'll tell you what.' Emily held up a hand to stem Stacey's interruption. 'He swanned off to France with a private allowance to lead a life of leisure playing at being an artist. Then he goes off on the quiet, gets married and has the nerve to grumble because you didn't drop everything to track him down after Dolly's sad news.'

'Emily, don't,' Stacey implored.

'Sorry.' Her friend hugged her. 'I don't mean to upset you, only it makes my blood boil. If Ben was here now I'd tell him exactly what I think of him and I wouldn't mince my words. How dare he threaten to throw you out on the street? By the way, there's always a bed in my place.'

'Thanks, Emily. Where would I be without you?'

'That's what friends are for. What's Rafe's take on all this by the way?'

'I haven't had a chance to speak to him.'

After leaving the solicitor's office,

Stacey had driven back to Normanswood alone. As a mark of respect to Max, Wade Manor had been closed for the day. Rafe hadn't said where he was going, but like Ben he hadn't lingered after the meeting was over.

Emily's eyes glanced at the letter Stacey had placed on the table.

'It's from Max,' she explained. 'He says he doesn't want me to do anything silly like give Ben half the proceeds of Wade Manor because I feel sorry for him.'

'There speaks the voice of sense,' Emily said.

'There's a lot of other stuff too.' Stacey re-folded the letter and put it behind an ornament, her focus beginning to blur. Max had told her how much he loved her and how foolish he'd been in his views on women in business. He'd asked for her forgiveness and assured her that his confidence in her ability wasn't misplaced.

'Did Rafe get anything?' Emily asked with interest.

'There was a small bequest and he had a letter too,' Stacey replied.

'Right. Well, I didn't come round to help you wallow in grief. I came round to suggest we have another night out.'

'I couldn't.' Stacey shook her head.

'I didn't mean right now, of course, but make a diary note of it. It's time you started to enjoy yourself. You've been working so hard, and it's not good for you.'

'I enjoy it,' Stacey retaliated.

'I enjoy my work too, but don't become a victim of your own success. There's life outside Wade Manor. Now what do you intend to do tonight?'

'I'm going to have a long, hot soak in the bath with some of Dolly's body oil.'

'Want me to stay over? I can easily sleep on the sofa.'

'No, I'll be fine, but thanks.'

'Then I'll see you in the morning. Helena sends all her love too. So do Charlie and Jack. See,' Emily beamed, 'you've got lots of friends, not to mention everyone at St Joseph's and all the members at the club.'

After Emily had gone, Stacey collapsed onto the sofa and reread Max's letter. As if sensing her distress, Lord jumped up beside her and rested his head on her knee. It was warm and soft and she snuggled into his body. Lady draped herself over Stacey's feet.

The ring at the front doorbell made them all jump. Lady quivered and Lord began to bark loudly. Stacey scrambled reluctantly to her feet.

'Rafe?' she greeted him with a nervous smile.

'I hope I'm not disturbing you,' he said, taking in her dishevelled appearance.

'I think I may have fallen asleep on the sofa.'

Rafe had changed out of his business suit into casual chinos and a polo shirt. Stacey blinked and ran a hand through her mussed hair. Her blouse was crumpled and her eye make-up felt streaked.

'Can we talk?' he asked.

It was then Stacey noticed that in contrast to his laid-back appearance, he was carrying a briefcase.

'Now?'

'If convenient.'

Back in the lounge, Rafe opened his briefcase and placed some papers on the coffee table.

'Is this a business meeting?' Stacey asked.

'I thought it would be better to discuss matters here rather than at the club.'

'Matters?' Stacey repeated carefully.

Rafe threw her an uncompromising look. 'After today's events you must realise changes will have to be made.'

'Yes, but I haven't had a chance to give them any thought.'

'Naturally I appreciate that, but I wanted to let you know my decision as soon as possible.'

'Decision?' Stacey echoed.

'Max's will changes everything between us.' Rafe paused. 'I presume you're not going to sell up?'

'Rafe,' Stacey remonstrated with him, 'I really haven't had time to think anything through.'

'My take is,' he ignored her interruption, 'that you don't sell up. It would be foolish to forsake everything we've worked for. Ben has put nothing into the business and I don't see why he should profit from all your hard work.'

'You worked hard too,' Stacey put in.

'I am not family,' Rafe replied, 'as was made evident in Max's letter to me.'

Rafe was seated close enough to Stacey for her to see a shadow of stubble on his cheek. Quelling an irrational urge to run her fingers over it, she forced herself to ask in a steady voice, 'May I be permitted to know what Max said to you?'

'He said he had made me the offer of chief executive officer as compensation for the misunderstanding with my father.'

'Go on,' Stacey urged.

'Because he felt bad about what

happened in the past and because he wanted to have someone he trusted in a position of authority at Wade Manor.'

Stacey nodded.

'He apologised for not telling me beforehand of his intention to make the deeds over to you, and he stressed the point that despite Ben's suspicions you had absolutely no idea of his intentions in that direction.'

'I was as taken aback as everyone else,' Stacey said.

'Effectively you are now in charge of everything.' Rafe cleared his throat. 'I think it's possible that Max cherished some romantic notion that we would somehow get together and everyone would live happily ever after, but we all know life isn't a fairy tale.'

'Rafe,' Stacey's voice quivered, 'what are you saying?'

'You are now the boss. In future all decisions will be up to you. Everything you need to know is in my briefcase. Confidential documents are stored in the safe.' An unreadable expression crossed Rafe's face. 'As I know the combination, and in view of past events, I would suggest you change it immediately.'

'For goodness sake, Rafe, couldn't all this wait?'

'No. I'm handing in my notice forthwith. I've checked out my contract and there is a get-out clause which I intend to invoke with immediate effect.'

'You can't walk out on me like this.'

'I think you'll find I can, and before you accuse me of acting in a fit of pique, that's not my intention at all. I've done the job I came to do. Wade Manor is thriving.'

'Max didn't intend you to leave.'

'Maybe not, but my work here is done.'

'What about us?' Stacey managed to ask.

'I think you'll agree,' Rafe said slowly, 'there is no us.' He stood up. 'I shan't be returning to Australia immediately. There are one or two things here I need to attend to should you need to contact me before I leave.'

In a corner of the room, as if sensing his departure, Lady whined.

Rafe's slow smile tore at Stacey's heart. Remembering his kisses and how kind he had been when Max had first fallen ill made a part of her long to throw herself into his arms. Tossing back her head, her determination of spirit rose to the fore. If Rafe wanted to leave, she certainly wasn't going to beg him to stay.

'Naturally I'll fall in with Max's wishes. I'm only sorry and surprised that you share his outdated prejudices.'

'What do you mean?'

'There was an excuse for Max. He came from a generation where the board of directors was totally male-dominated. I would have thought someone like you would have moved with the times, but I've learned a lot about the male sex today. My step-brother thinks I wormed my way into Max's affections in order to inherit his business empire, and you feel you cannot work under a woman.' It gave Stacey small pleasure to see Rafe flinch as if she had slapped his face.

'That's not how it is at all.'

'The end result is the same. You've terminated your contract and you're leaving. Now if you'll excuse me, I'd better acquaint myself with the contents of your briefcase if I'm going to be flying solo in future.' She sat down on the sofa. 'Can you see yourself out?'

17

Normanswood had never looked more beautiful. The common was bathed in early evening sunlight and the smell of newly mown grass lingered on the air. All the trees were in bud, waiting to burst forth into blossom.

Stacey kicked at some loose grass cuttings, a childhood indulgence that had never left her. She smiled as she remembered how cross her mother had been when some friends had long ago buried her in the loose grass as part of a game and then wouldn't reveal where she was hidden. It had taken her mother ages to find Stacey, who had completely forgotten she had been invited to a party. It had also taken Iris forever to get the grass out of her daughter's hair and to make her presentable for the birthday party. As for the clothes Stacey had been wearing, they had been stained beyond redemption and consigned to the dustbin.

Stacey wished she could hide under the cuttings again now and let the world get on without her, but hiding away wasn't an option. Neither was it her style. Word had spread like wildfire through the village. Everyone had been talking about her legacy and the abrupt departure of Rafe Stocker. Helena had been agog for news when Stacey had arrived for work the morning following the reading of the will. Stacey had provided her with the sketchiest of details, not wishing to air in public her family differences. Many of the female members of the club had been devastated by the news. Rafe was a popular person. He knew exactly how far to go in teasing the ladies, without incurring any unpleasantness from either their partners or the other members. Every day Stacey heard a new story of his kindness and consideration, especially to the children of St Joseph's, who received the news of his departure in unusually hushed tones before their morning swimming session.

Stacey hoped Rafe's departure wouldn't prompt a flood of cancelled memberships.

★ ★ ★

'I don't know how to tell you this,' Helena began after Stacey had explained that Rafe was intending to eventually return to Australia.

'It's not Toni, is it?' Stacey asked in concern. 'She was making such good progress.'

'Toni's fine,' Helena said with her beautiful smile. 'The doctors are pleased with her progress. They're confidently predicting she'll be given the all clear soon.'

'That's wonderful news,' Stacey replied. 'We must throw a party for her to celebrate.'

'The thing is . . . ' Helena pulled a face.

'What is it?'

'We may not be here.'

'Don't tell me you're leaving too.'

'Charlie's been offered a job. It's in Wales. He's been out of work for so long, he had almost given up hope of ever getting another one. He wants to move up there as soon as possible.' Helena cleared her throat. 'As you know, the girls' father lives in Wales, and well . . . it all made sense. They would be able to see him more often and with Toni on the way to recovery, there's little to keep me here.'

'You're going to live with Charlie in Wales?' Stacey could hardly believe what she was hearing.

'He's asked me to marry him.' Helena hesitated, then taking a deep breath, she added, 'And I've said yes. Of course I wouldn't dream of leaving you in the lurch, and I had no idea Rafe was thinking of leaving too. If it's inconvenient I could always change my plans.'

'I wouldn't dream of asking you to do

any such thing,' Stacey insisted. 'I needed cheering up and your news has done exactly that. I can't remember when I was so pleased.' Stacey hugged Helena. 'Everybody seems to be getting married,' she laughed. 'It must be something in the air.'

'There's so much to arrange, so we wouldn't be moving immediately, but I'm thinking perhaps halfway through the summer? I know that would be leaving you at one of our busiest times, but I would be around to help my replacement for a little while. I could show him or her the ropes and I'd be at the end of a telephone line if there was a real problem.'

'I shall miss you dreadfully,' Stacey admitted, only now realising how much Helena's friendship and support meant to her.

'You'll always be welcome in Wales,' she said. 'I want your promise that you will visit.'

'You have it,' Stacey said.

'I did think at one time,' Helena said

slowly, 'that you and Rafe — ?' she let the question dangle in the air.

'We have absolutely no plans in that direction,' Stacey replied.

'There never was anything between us,' Helena began to explain, 'apart from friendship. I mean I know that in the beginning you had your suspicions about us, but we were only good friends.'

'I realise that,' Stacey replied, 'but the relationship between you and Rafe has got absolutely nothing to do with my relationship with him. Now, I suppose we had better get on with some work.'

★ ★ ★

Stacey did a few limbering up exercises on the common as she watched the dog walkers and the children playing on the swings. They looked so carefree. She wished she could join them, but she had a feeling the warden wouldn't be too pleased if she did.

Stacey's fitness routine had lapsed

due to the recent pressures of work, and she enjoyed the feel of stretching her limbs again. She began to pound the path that circuited the common. Her breath came in short, sharp bursts and she realised how unfit she had become. She very much doubted she would be able to complete the mini-marathon course any more without some serious training.

Her thoughts turned to Ben as she jogged along. Since he had returned to France, she had heard nothing from him, and not wanting to have another scene she hadn't rung him either. A visit to the bank had confirmed her suspicion that there was no way she could raise funds to purchase Stopes Cottage off him at the current market price. The thought of leaving filled her with dread. She had lived there ever since her mother's marriage to Max and it had been the family home for many years before that. Every morning she awoke fearing she would find a 'for sale' notice on a board outside.

Dolly had telephoned several times. Stacey hadn't wanted to burden her with all that had gone on between herself and Ben. She didn't know how much Dolly suspected. The older woman could at times be very astute and it wouldn't take much for her to wheedle the full story out of Stacey. For this reason Stacey had turned down her regular invitations to fly out to Menorca for a short break, citing work as the reason.

'You're in danger of turning into a Stacey No Mates,' Dolly had complained. 'Can't you take pity on a lonely stepmother? We could indulge in another massage?'

'I will visit as soon as I can,' Stacey promised.

'I'll hold you to that,' Dolly replied before ringing off.

Stacey had now left the common and the country lane adjacent grew narrower, causing cow parsley to swish against her legs. She jogged into the road, keeping an ear out for approaching vehicles. In

251

the distance she could hear a farm vehicle in a far field. Startled by a cow whose head suddenly appeared through a gap in the hedge, Stacey lost her footing. She shrieked, then grinned at the startled animal that looked equally as shocked to see her.

'Hi there.' Stacey leaned over and tickled her nose with some long grass. The cow shied away and loped off to the far end of the field. Stacey sighed. No one, it seemed, wanted to talk to her these days.

She increased her pace and to lift her spirits began to sing an old marching song Max had taught her and Ben during one of their camping holidays. She matched her pace to her erratic singing, rather pleased when she reached a high note. There was no one around apart from the cows and she belted out the number at the top of her voice. She'd read somewhere that singing released tensions, and she had to agree it was a long time since she'd felt this liberated.

She closed her eyes for a second to concentrate on the final note. A loud blast of a car horn behind her caught her totally by surprise and the next moment she was face-down in a ditch, her right arm buckled agonisingly beneath her.

'Stacey?' she heard a voice through the mist of pain. 'Are you all right?'

All she could manage was a groan.

'Can you move?' There was new urgency in the voice. 'On second thought, stay where you are. I'll call an ambulance.'

'The x-ray shows you've a badly sprained wrist,' the doctor in A & E advised Stacey. 'You're lucky not to have broken any bones.'

'I can't move my hand,' Stacey complained.

'That's the idea of a support bandage. Now I prescribe complete rest.'

'No, you don't understand,' Stacey began.

'I'll see she gets some rest,' a clipped voice cut in.

'You'll do no such thing.' Stacey glared at Rafe. 'It's your fault I'm in this position.'

'Then it's up to me to put things right between us, isn't it?' he countered. 'If you've finished here, Doctor?'

'I have,' he said, adding with a rueful smile, 'good luck with the patient. I've a feeling you'll have your hands full.'

After thanking him, Stacey allowed Rafe to help her into his car as carefully as if she was a delicate piece of china. Her arm was beginning to throb and she was grateful for his support, although wild horses would not have dragged the statement from her.

'There's no need to tuck a blanket around my legs,' she protested.

'Warmth is good for shock.' Rafe got into the driver's seat and started the engine.

'What made you sound your horn like that?' Stacey demanded.

'You were prancing around all over the place like a demented dragoon. What on earth were you doing?'

'If you must know, I was singing.'

'Is that what you call it? You half scared the cows out of their wits.'

'Come to that, what were you doing driving around country lanes?'

'The main road is closed for resurfacing. You're lucky it's a short cut known only by the locals, otherwise you'd have probably encountered more cars and we could have had a traffic situation on our hands.'

'Since when have you been a local?' Stacey demanded.

'I'm not really,' Rafe admitted. 'I keep forgetting. Everyone's made me so welcome.'

'And you've repaid them by running back home at the first opportunity.'

Rafe turned up the heating to take the chill off the evening air. 'Do you think we could call a temporary truce to the hostilities?' he asked with a smile.

Stacey looked across at Rafe, not wanting to admit how much she was going to miss his company.

'If you like,' she agreed slowly.

'Good, because it looks like we're going to be working closely together again.'

'What do you mean?'

Rafe nodded at her bandaged arm. 'I take it you've no intention of going sick?'

'I never go sick,' Stacey replied.

'Much as I thought,' Rafe said. 'As I'm partially responsible for your injury,' he began.

'Make that totally responsible.'

'And as your movements will be severely restricted for a few days, I feel I ought to make amends.'

'Supposing I don't want you to?'

'How are you going to manage? You won't be able to drive or operate a computer, and you'll have difficulty dressing yourself.'

'I won't need your help on that one,' Stacey was quick to put in.

'I agree, but I can help with the other duties.'

'What about your flight to Australia?'

'I haven't finalised my plans yet.'

Rafe flicked an indicator switch and drew into the parking space at the end of Lavender Lane. 'Here we are. Now, dinner? I have a fancy for some fish and chips and from the smell of things,' he sniffed, 'the local chippy appears to be open.'

Clutching two warm newspaper parcels, they trudged up the lane to Stopes Cottage. It looked warm and welcoming in the half-light and Stacey's breath caught in her chest as she again thought of the wrench of moving.

'Looks like you've got visitors,' Rafe said.

'I'm not expecting anybody.'

'The lights are on and the front door's open too. You'd better let me go first. We don't want your other wrist damaged. Hello?' he called out. 'Anybody there?'

Stacey bumped into Rafe's back as he came to a halt. The door to the living room opened slowly. With their tails wagging, Lord and Lady romped out to greet them.

'Not for you.' Rafe held his fish out of the reach of their enquiring noses.

'So there you are,' a voice behind them said. 'Don't look so surprised to see me.'

'Ben?' Stacey demanded. 'What are you doing here?'

'I'm perfectly entitled to be here,' he pointed out. 'It's my house and I've come home to discuss plans for putting it up for sale.'

18

'You can't do that,' Stacey exploded.

'I can do what I like with my own property,' Ben fired straight back at her. 'I've already visited some agents.'

'You could at least have talked things through with me first.' The throbbing in Stacey's wrist was making her feel sick and she also began to feel dizzy now the effect of the painkillers was wearing off.

Lord and Lady began barking and running around in circles, swishing their tails in anguish. Raised voices still made them nervous and the hall was soon a scene of uproar as everyone tried to speak at the same time.

'I suggest,' Rafe said as he positioned himself between Ben and Stacey, 'that we all calm down.'

Ben glared at Rafe. 'This is none of your business.'

'That's as may be, but can't you see

your sister's been in an accident, Ben? Arguments of this nature are the last thing she needs.'

The expression on Ben's face changed in an instant, as he noticed Stacey's injury.

'What sort of accident?' he demanded. 'Stace? Are you OK?' His earlier belligerence disappeared in an instant. 'You've gone ever so pale. You're not going to faint on us, are you? Here, let me get you a chair. Why didn't you say? Is this anything to do with you?' He gave Rafe another glare. 'Because if it is, you'll have me to answer to.'

'Why don't we discuss details in the kitchen?' Rafe suggested, not looking in the least intimidated by Ben's threats.

'Yes, come on, Stace.' Ben placed a solicitous arm around Stacey's shoulders and began gently guiding her along the hall and into the kitchen.

'There's hardly room to move here.'

'And I need to warm these up in the

oven.' Rafe indicated their fish supper parcels.

Ben's face lit up at the sight of food. 'Is that what I think it is? Great, I'm starving. That's one thing the French can't cook, good old-fashioned cod and chips. Here, sit down, Stace.' He drew out one of the kitchen chairs and, plonking her down on the cushioned seat, snatched the parcels out of Rafe's hands and headed towards the oven. Stacey raised her eyebrows at Rafe.

'Bit of luck I ordered double portions, I think,' Rafe murmured in a low voice.

'What am I going to do?' Stacey demanded, her mind on more important things than food as her head began to clear. 'He's going to sell Stopes Cottage.'

'All in good time,' Rafe insisted. 'First we need to eat.'

The tension eased as Rafe sorted out drinks and ordered Ben to set the table. Opening the back door, he nudged the two dogs towards the night air. 'Go on, shoo,' he urged them outside.

'What happened?' Ben nodded towards Stacey's wrist.

'I had an argument with a ditch,' she explained with a rueful smile, 'and I'll have another with you if you think I'm going to faint.'

Ben squeezed the fingers of her good hand.

'Sorry, I shouldn't have come at you like that, but I've been a bit under pressure recently and I know you never faint. Yvette sends her love by the way.'

'How is she?'

'Under pressure like the rest of us, but don't worry, we'll work something out.'

Soon the kitchen was cosy with the smell of the chips browning in the oven.

'If you're not going to finish yours, I'll have them,' Ben said to Stacey, whose appetite wasn't up to doing justice to the generous serving Rafe had placed before her.

She passed over her plate and took a

sip of the wine Rafe had poured out for her.

'I think you owe your sister a proper apology,' Rafe said as Ben finally finished eating, 'for all the distress you've caused her.'

Ben, his face flushed from the heat of the kitchen, blinked at Rafe, then turned to look at Stacey.

'Sorry, Stace,' he mumbled, 'but you've got to see things from my point of view. We've over-extended ourselves. Yvette's ambitious. She's got plans and,' he shrugged, 'we need the money.'

Stacey nodded, too exhausted to argue her case further. 'Do you want me to move out now?'

'Of course not. Look,' he cast a glance at Rafe, 'perhaps we ought to discuss this in private?'

'No.' Stacey put out her good arm and pinioned Rafe's hand to the table. 'I want Rafe to stay.'

'So it's like that between you two is it? I thought there was something going on.'

Rafe squeezed Stacey's fingers and, shaking his head, threw her a warning glance that brought the colour back to her cheeks.

'But I was under the impression you were going back to Australia.' Ben frowned.

'There's been a slight change of plan,' Rafe replied. 'My departure could be delayed indefinitely,' he added.

Ben looked from Rafe to Stacey then back to Rafe again.

'I am missing something here, aren't I?' he demanded.

'Your sister is going to need help. Her wrist has been badly sprained. The last thing she wants is you coming in here thrusting estate agent details under her nose.'

'I admit my timing could have been better, but these things can't wait. The sooner we get the cottage on the market, the sooner it can be sold and we can all move on with our lives. It should fetch a good price. These bijou properties are very fashionable right now. I've made an appointment for someone to come and measure up and take photos.'

The dogs, wanting to be let back in, began to scratch at the door.

'I'll move out as soon as I can,' Stacey said. 'Will next week be early enough?'

'You'll do no such thing,' Rafe said.

'Stop ordering my sister around.' Ben stood up and did his best to loom over Rafe, but Lady, having finally managed to nudge open the latch on the door on her own, bounded into the kitchen and entwined her lissom body around his legs, causing him to topple against the cooker with a loud crash. While he was busy trying to disentangle himself, Rafe took the opportunity to thrust some sweet biscuits towards Stacey. 'Have one of these,' he insisted, extracting a pink sugary confection from the packet. 'You know sugar is good for shock.'

'I don't like pink wafer biscuits,' she objected.

'You don't have a choice.'

'Get off me,' Ben shouted, now pinioned against the cooker as Lord joined Lady in the kitchen and began to lick his hand.

Seeing the determination in Rafe's eyes, Stacey took one of the biscuits; then, feeling light-headed, she began to laugh at the ridiculous sight of Ben in combat with the two dogs.

'Don't you dare slap my face,' she said, jerking away from Rafe's open palm. 'I'm not hysterical.'

'Get these animals away from me, Stace. I need help.'

'What on earth is going on here?' a voice demanded from the back door that had been left open by the dogs.

Deserting Ben, they bounded over to greet the new arrival.

'Dolly,' Stacey coughed as she nearly choked on her biscuit.

'I've been ringing the bell and hammering on the front door for hours.' She smiled at Stacey. 'Maybe that's a slight exaggeration, but when I realised no one could hear me I followed the sound of barking dogs. Now do I get a welcome kiss?' She held out her arms. 'My poor lamb. What have you done to your hand?' she demanded as she spotted Stacey's sling. 'Are you responsible for this?' she accused Ben.

'No.' With a singular lack of gallantry, Ben pointed towards Rafe. 'He is.'

'I think,' Dolly said as she came into the kitchen, 'I'll have some of that wine.'

Rafe poured her out a glass. 'Thank you,' she said. 'Now, who's going to update me on all that's been happening?'

Ensconced in the lounge and seated on the sofa beside Dolly, Stacey began to feel marginally better. Dolly insisted she lean back and rest against the cushions.

'I don't know what these men have been doing to you,' she complained, 'but you looked washed out.'

'Thanks, Dolly. You certainly know how to make a girl feel good.'

'You need some feminine tender loving care and I intend to provide it.'

The dogs, becalmed by Dolly's soothing voice, settled at Stacey's feet.

'Now.' Dolly adjusted her glasses and, looking as though she was about to chair a board meeting, took a long hard look at Rafe and Ben. Stacey stifled another fit of the giggles, which she hastily turned into a cough, earning her a baleful look from Ben.

'You first.' Dolly nodded towards Rafe.

If Rafe objected to being treated like an office boy, he gave no indication of it. He and Dolly had only met once at Max's memorial service and as far as Stacey could remember they hadn't exchanged more than half a dozen words. Dolly had left almost immediately after the ceremony and Rafe had said he had some work to do, even though Wade Manor had been closed for the day.

'As you can see, Stacey injured her wrist,' he began.

'Because you knocked her into a ditch,' Ben seized his chance to point out.

'Your turn will come later,' Dolly reprimanded him. 'Go on.' She turned back to Rafe.

'I've decided to rearrange my plans to return to Australia. Stacey is going to need help.'

'If you recall, we hadn't actually come to a decision,' Stacey objected.

'With her mobility impaired she may have problems with some of her day-to-day tasks,' Rafe carried on.

'It strikes me you should never have walked out on my stepdaughter in the first place,' Dolly remarked. 'As for you,' she said, turning to Ben, 'What's all this about?' She held up one of the estate agent brochures Ben had thrust at Stacey.

'As you know, my father left me this cottage,' he began.

'Which you are intending to sell?'

'I had hoped to have a private talk with Stacey, but so far all that's happened is I've been accused of throwing her out of the family home to reclaim what is rightfully mine.'

'Your behaviour is disgraceful, young man,' Dolly said.

'He's perfectly within his rights, Dolly,' Stacey spoke up for Ben.

'I thought I told you to rest.' Her harsh words were tempered with her sweet smile. 'You've done more than enough to get the business back on its feet and it's time these two recognised that fact. There's no need for you to stay on if you have pressing issues in the Antipodes.' She addressed her next remark to Rafe. 'I shall stay and look after Stacey's personal needs.'

'Wade Manor is no concern of yours,' Rafe said firmly.

'From what you say, neither is it any concern of yours, but,' Dolly went on, 'I am prepared to accept you know all there is to know about running the business.'

'I'm glad we agree on one thing at least,' Rafe said gravely with just the suggestion of a wink at Stacey. 'I take it then that I have your permission to stay?'

'If Stacey is agreeable to your plans then I won't object.'

'Then that just leaves the issue of Stopes Cottage.' Rafe looked at Ben. 'Have you actually commissioned an agent to handle the sale?'

'Look,' Ben shifted uncomfortably in his seat, 'I didn't realise it would cause this much hassle. I'm sure Yvette and I can work something out. You can stay, Stace, for as long as you like. I couldn't sleep easy in my bed knowing I'd turned you out.'

'I'm prepared to buy it off you at market price.'

Three pairs of eyes turned in Rafe's direction.

'What did you say?' Stacey demanded.

'I'm making an offer for Stopes Cottage.'

'You're not serious.' Twin spots of colour stained Ben's cheeks.

271

'I think it's an excellent idea,' Dolly said.

'At the risk of sounding impolite, Dolly,' Ben addressed his stepmother, 'it's none of your business.'

'You can discuss the details later.' Dolly ignored Ben's interruption. 'There, that's one problem sorted. Now before you start up again about being short of funds, Ben, I have another proposal. And I would suggest you curb your tongue, otherwise I may have to rethink what I have in mind.'

Ben turned pink, then after a brief battle with his conscience nodded his head.

'Good. Now I would like to invest in this art project business thing of yours.'

'You what?' Ben gasped.

'Of course I would have to come out and visit to see exactly what I'm putting my money into.'

'Dolly, that's a step too far.' Stacey leaned across the sofa, wondering how she could tactfully dissuade the older woman from investing her money in what could prove to be an expensive white elephant. 'Ben's had these ideas before.'

'I know in the past they haven't exactly worked out as planned, but Yvette's the brains behind this one, Stace,' Ben butted in.

'I'm pleased to hear it,' Dolly replied. 'Good. That's all settled then.'

'One moment.' Ben held up a hand. 'Could you run that past me again?'

'I thought I made myself perfectly clear.'

'I want to make sure I understood you.'

'You are in need of funds and I am prepared to help out, provided we can reach an agreement.'

'Why?' Ben asked the question on everyone's mind.

'Hardly the response I was looking for, darling.'

'That's as may be, but you don't have to do this, Dolly. I'm not your responsibility,' Ben pointed out.

Dolly fell unaccountably silent for a few moments.

'Dolly?' Stacey prompted, fearing Ben's straight talking might have hurt her feelings.

'I'm lonely,' Dolly admitted in a quiet voice. 'When Max came into my life I realised how much I'd missed being involved in a family. He filled the void. I was overjoyed to inherit two stepchildren and when we lost him,' she began sniffing loudly before groping in her capacious bag for a tissue, 'I didn't know what to do. Going out to lunch every day with friends, then playing eternal rounds of golf — a game I've never really enjoyed — didn't do it for me. I needed a purpose. When you didn't take me up on my invite to come out and visit, Stacey,' she threw her a shamefaced smile, 'I decided to come and visit you. If you think I'm being an interfering old woman, don't hesitate to tell me.' She threw her head back. 'I can take it on the chin.'

Forgetting about her injured wrist,

Stacey threw her arms around Dolly's neck.

'You are an interfering old woman,' she agreed with a laugh, 'but I love you all the more for it. You can carry on interfering as long as you like. I won't mind.'

'Neither will I,' Ben agreed, getting up and kissing her on cheek, 'if you really meant what you said about our art project.'

'You may live to regret those words,' Dolly warned him as she disentangled herself from the pair of them and tried to sound gruff. 'Thank goodness your wife sounds a sensible young woman. I look forward to meeting her.'

'Any time you like.'

Dolly turned to Rafe. 'Do you have a spare bedroom in your flat above the wool shop?'

A look of alarm spread across Rafe's face. 'You're not thinking of spending the night with me?'

'No, but Ben is.'

'I'm staying here,' Ben protested.

'This is my house.'

'Something you keep reminding us of with boring repetition. However, I intend to stay here.' The look she threw Ben dared him to contradict her. 'I seem to recall the third bedroom is no bigger than a box room.'

'It was Ben's room, Dolly,' Stacey pointed out.

'And the last time I looked it was full of rubbish. Do you fancy clearing it out tonight? I thought not.'

'Agreed. Ben can stay over with me.' Rafe rose to his feet. 'And before we both outstay our welcome, I suggest we leave. Stacey seems to have difficulty keeping her eyes open.' He leaned forward and, ignoring the speculative look that passed between Ben and Dolly, kissed her gently on the fore-head. 'Don't let her bully you,' he warned in a soft voice.

'I heard that and as if I would,' Dolly objected. 'Now off you go the pair of you. We'll catch up tomorrow.'

Dolly saw the two men to the door,

then came back into the sitting room.

'I approve of that young man,' she announced.

'Ben?'

'There's nothing wrong with your brother that a good woman won't put right. No, I was referring to Rafe. I hope you're not going to let him slip through your fingers?'

'Dolly.' Already Stacey was beginning to regret her open invitation for her to stay as long as she liked. 'He has already broken the terms of his contract. As soon as I'm fully mobile he is going back to Australia. There's no place in my life for Rafe Stocker.'

'Then you'd better tell him that yourself tomorrow morning.'

'Dolly,' Stacey asked with a hint of suspicion, 'what have you done?'

'I've invited him over for a one-to-one with you here in Stopes Cottage. Don't worry, I won't be here. Ben and I will be Skyping with Yvette. We also have business to discuss. Heavens, is that the time? Off you go to bed. I'll be up to help you when I've tidied the mess in the kitchen and settled the dogs down for the night.'

The cottage creaked comfortably as Stacey made her way upstairs, her mind in a whirl. If Rafe was serious about buying Stopes Cottage, did that mean he also intended to stay in Normanswood? Why had he changed his mind?

Downstairs she heard Dolly humming happily to herself in the kitchen. Too tired to care what anyone's plans were for the future, Stacey headed for her bedroom.

19

After a fortifying breakfast of creamy scrambled eggs, buttery toast and homemade marmalade, washed down with strong breakfast tea, Dolly insisted Stacey sit out in the sunshine while she did the washing up and attended to some other household chores.

'You can't possibly do any good with that bandage around your wrist. It'll be just as quick for me to do everything on my own. Now off you go. I intend to see you obey the doctor's orders.'

Resigning herself to losing this battle, Stacey took the dogs for a quick leg stretch in the fields over the back before returning to Stopes Cottage to find Rafe had already arrived. He and Dolly were seated in the garden chairs chatting together.

'Right, well, I'm off,' Dolly announced as the squeaky garden gate alerted her to Stacey's return. 'I've laid out a tray of coffee cups and a plate of almond biscuits. See you eat them,' she insisted, 'and I want no nonsense about expanding waistlines. Fancy putting my girl on a fitness regime,' she berated Rafe, who looked suitably abashed.

'We did raise a huge amount for charity,' he attempted to justify himself, 'and Stacey would have come in first if she hadn't played the lady and held back to marshal the stragglers.'

Stacey looked at Rafe in surprise. Until that moment she'd had no idea that Rafe knew of her subterfuge.

'Hm.' Dolly made a sceptical noise at the back of her throat. 'All the same, I don't approve of diets unless it's for medical reasons, and there's nothing wrong with Stacey's health. Now, have you got everything you need?' she asked Stacey.

'I'll be here if she needs help,' Rafe

reminded Dolly.

'There are certain things a female doesn't like to ask a man,' Dolly said with a prim pursing of her lips. 'Lipstick and such like,' she added vaguely.

'I've got my handbag here with me.' Stacey indicated where it was stashed under the garden table. 'So if I feel a pressing need to renew my makeup I think I can cope.'

'Do you think you can manage to make the coffee?' Dolly turned her attack on Rafe. 'The milk's in the fridge and the jug kettle is full of water. Do you know how to work it?'

'I daresay I'll manage,' Rafe replied solemnly. 'Did you leave out the book of instructions in case it's too much of a challenge?'

'Don't be impertinent,' Dolly retaliated. 'I'm only trying to help.'

'And I've only sprained my wrist,' Stacey complained. 'I wish the two of you wouldn't keep treating me like an invalid.'

'I'm trying to make amends,' Rafe said. 'I feel responsible for what happened.'

'So you should,' Dolly remonstrated with him. 'I expect you were driving too fast down that country lane. Men always do. It's a form of showing off. Pathetic, I call it. We females don't feel the need for this supremacy thing. We know we're the superior sex.'

'Have you ever thought of taking up politics for a living, Dolly?' Stacey enquired, having great difficulty in keeping a straight face.

'Heaven help the opposition if she does,' murmured Rafe out the corner of his mouth.

'Am I going to have to wait all day?' Ben strolled out onto the terrace. 'The traffic warden's hovering and she's been by twice. As it is, I'm parked in an unloading bay. I hope the florist's isn't expecting a delivery of flowers.'

'Sorry, dear. Just coming.'

'Hi, Stace.' He smiled at his sister.

'Did you have a good night's sleep?'

She kissed Ben on the cheek, glad to see he was smiling and didn't look at though he was going to start on at her again about her squatting in his property.

'Not too bad.'

'That's more than I did. Your spare bed is incredibly lumpy,' he complained to Rafe, 'and there was an awful racket from the bikers who congregated outside.'

'I presume you want to borrow my car for the day?' Rafe dangled his keys just out of Ben's reach.

'Ben's going to chauffeur me around today,' Dolly explained to Stacey. 'I need to do some shopping. My clothes are too Spanish for the English climate and Rafe has very kindly agreed to lend us his car. Hand over the keys, Rafe, and stop teasing Ben.'

'Don't forget the business side of things,' Ben quickly reminded Dolly.

'I can't wait to meet my new daughter-in-law,' she confided to Stacey, 'even if it is on a computer screen. Now come along, Ben. Stacey and Rafe don't want us hanging around the place. They need to be alone.'

Along with everyone else, Ben obeyed Dolly's command. Pulling a comical face behind her back, he meekly followed her out to the car, promising Rafe he'd bring Dolly and the car back in one piece.

'Would you like some coffee?' Stacey asked when they'd gone.

'Later perhaps,' Rafe replied. 'Where shall we talk?' he asked, getting straight down to business.

'I'm not really sure what we need to talk about,' Stacey stalled.

Rafe glanced up at the sky to where some dark clouds lurked ominously on the horizon. 'We could be in for a shower. Let's go indoors.'

Stacey settled in an armchair, leaving Rafe perched on the edge of the sofa. 'You've brought your briefcase,' she said in surprise.

'It isn't full of money, if that's what's

worrying you.' Rafe undid the catch. A flush of colour stained Stacey's neck. Would he never let her forget her unjustified outburst?

'I know your father was innocent of all charges.' She chose her words carefully. 'I apologise for mistrusting you. What I said was unforgivable. I know Max wanted to apologise to your father, but he left it too late.'

'I'm sure my father knew,' Rafe replied, 'and if it's any consolation he loved the Australian way of life and I don't suppose he would have been motivated to emigrate if he hadn't been pushed.'

'I ought to telephone the club,' Stacey said, anxious to change the subject, 'to explain why I won't be in today.'

'No need. Helena and Charlie assure me they have got everything under control. Emily's on duty too, and they've promised to call me if there are any problems.'

'For someone who has handed in his

notice, you seem to have taken a lot on yourself.' Stacey's resentment bristled to the surface.

'I thought we agreed last night that while you're incapacitated it was business as usual?'

Stacey leaned back against a cushion. Despite what she'd told Dolly and Ben, she had suffered an interrupted night's sleep. So many thoughts had been raging in her head she hadn't been able to relax, and despite the painkillers her wrist throbbed every time she moved.

'Where is our relationship going?' she asked Rafe.

'Nowhere, I hope,' he replied with a smile.

'It's time for straight talking,' Stacey insisted. 'There's been far too much done behind my back. It's time for change.'

'Very well.' Rafe stopped smiling. 'Ben and I talked things through last night regarding Stopes Cottage and we've come to an agreement. As soon

as we can, we'll contact our solicitors
and get a contract drawn up.'

'You really are buying it then?'

'Subject to all the usual rules and
regulations, that would seem to be the
idea.'

'When do you want me to move out?'

'I don't.'

Stacey winced as pain stabbed her in
the wrist.

'What was that?'

'I'll come back to it, but first there's
something you should read.' Rafe held
up a piece of paper.

'What is it?' Stacey asked.

'Max's letter, the one the solicitor
gave me.'

'Isn't it private?'

'Max expressed the wish that I
would stay on at Wade Manor, despite
his decision to leave the business to
you.'

'Is that why you immediately opted
out of your contract in order to return
to Australia?'

Rafe made a gesture with his hands.

'Not my finest hour, I admit. It was actually a bit of stiff-necked Aussie pride. I suppose you could say I felt I had been elbowed out. Max had placed all his trust in me and then he repaid that trust by cutting me out of everything. I'm not saying I wanted to benefit from his will — far from it — but the idea of losing Wade Manor was more than I could bear.'

'So you decided if you couldn't have it all you'd have none of it?'

'Harsh words, but there's a grain of truth in them.'

'Perhaps now you'll understand how I felt when I learned of Max's plans to appoint you as chief executive officer?'

'Perhaps I do,' Rafe echoed softly.

'Does your purchase of Stopes Cottage mean you've changed your mind about staying on?'

'Do you want me to stay on?'

Stacey struggled to keep her composure. If this was going to be the most important conversation of her life, she didn't want to get things wrong.

'Are you saying you're prepared to come back to Wade Manor to work?'

'If the conditions are acceptable.'

'If we're going to work together we need to do so on an equal footing,' Stacey replied.

'What exactly did you have in mind?' Rafe asked.

Stacey cleared her throat. 'As far as I can see it, the only way we could enjoy equal status would be as man and wife.'

'And?' Rafe prompted.

'Would you be prepared to consider getting married?'

'To you?'

'Yes,' Stacey swallowed. 'Only as a business arrangement,' she added.

After a few moments Rafe said, 'My answer has to be no.' His reply hit Stacey with all the force of a body blow to the stomach.

'I expected that would be your answer,' she admitted in a hollow voice.

'Is there no way we can work things out?'

'There is Stopes Cottage.'

'I suppose you'll want to move in as soon as possible?'

'I think Dolly might have something to say on that score,' Rafe replied.

'I'll move out as soon as I've found somewhere else.'

'That won't be necessary.'

'What do you suggest I do then?' Stacey's eyes crashed into Rafe's. For a man who had just turned down a proposal of marriage, he was looking at her in a manner of marked approval, one she found extremely disturbing.

'I suggest we get married.'

'You said you weren't prepared to consider the idea.'

'Only as a business arrangement.'

'What?'

'I know; it came at me like a bolt out of the blue too.'

'What did?'

'The last thing on my mind when I took up Max's offer of a job was falling in love. Especially not with his step-daughter, who couldn't get out of bed in the morning and was late for his birthday lunch.'

'We've already been through all that,' Stacey retorted, 'and since we're into plain speaking, I certainly wasn't enamoured with you.'

'Really?' Rafe raised an eyebrow.

'No girl likes to be informed she's spoilt, unfit, inefficient, can't hold down a job, and I can't remember what else you said about me, but give me time and I will.'

'I'd stop right there if I were you,' Rafe cut in.

'Why?'

'Because I want to kiss you.'

'No.' Stacey jerked upright.

'Why not? I've done it twice before. Didn't you enjoy it?'

'That's beside the point.'

'I don't think so. If you want my take, I enjoyed it thoroughly and I'd rather like to do it again, unless of course you're going to go all maidenly on me and insist we get engaged before we indulge in that sort of activity.'

'Now what are you talking about?' Stacey's head was swimming.

'You've got to remember I'm a colonial. We don't always know how to behave in these circumstances. I've got friends whose idea of sophistication is salt on the chips.'

'Stop, please.'

'Do you know why I was driving down that country lane last night? No? Then I'll tell you. I was plucking up the courage to come and see you.'

'Why?'

'To see if you wanted to marry me.'

'You turned down my proposal.'

'Only the business side of things. You know, I thought I was imagining things when you suddenly appeared from nowhere, singing a tuneless song and looking absolutely beautiful.'

'No.' Stacey shook her hands in a gesture of negativity.

'You're not turning me down now,

are you?' Rafe leaned forward.

'Yes. No. I don't know.'

'You don't understand. I don't think I can live without you.'

'I can't live without you either.' The words were out before Stacey realised what she had said.

'Then what are you saying no for?'

'We're totally unsuited.'

'Who says?' Rafe's voice was now a rough rasp in her ear.

'You're a macho Aussie male. I'll be your boss. We don't agree on anything. What sort of future would that make for us?'

'It should make for a heady and vibrant mix, wouldn't you say? Our life together would never be dull.'

'Do you really want to marry me — properly?'

'I've never been surer of anything in my life.'

'Why?'

'I suppose you want all the dirty details? Here goes then.' Rafe took a deep breath. 'I love the way you were determined not to let me get the better of you. I saw the light in your eyes when you were longing to deck me one and on occasions I can't say I would have blamed you.'

'You don't know how close I came to it.'

'I can guess. But you didn't give in, did you?'

'I've got my fair share of stiff-necked pride too,' Stacey said.

'Everyone was deserting the ship — me, Helena, Ben. You thought you were going to lose Stopes Cottage into the bargain, but you never once considered giving up, did you?'

'I couldn't,' Stacey admitted.

'May I ask when you decided to fall in love with me? Or am I presuming too much?'

'When I fell into that wretched ditch,' Stacey admitted.

'That wasn't part of my technique,' Rafe admitted, his eyes widening in surprise.

'Whatever. It worked.' Stacey rested

her head on Rafe's shoulder.

'Shall we stop talking for a while?' he suggested.

'Why?'

'Because I can think of much better things to do.'

'Dolly.' Stacey shoved Rafe in the chest.

'She's not back already, is she?' Rafe cast a glance over his shoulder. 'I told Ben to keep her occupied all day.'

'Do you realise if we get married, that you'll have her for a mother-in-law?'

'There's a price to pay for everything,' Rafe replied with a rueful smile. 'I think it's one I'm prepared to accept.'

'Will you break the news to her, or shall I?' Stacey asked.

'Make a diary note and we'll discuss it later, boss,' Rafe said before his lips descended on hers.

We do hope that you have enjoyed reading this large print book.

Did you know that all of our titles are available for purchase?

We publish a wide range of high quality large print books including:
Romances, Mysteries, Classics
General Fiction
Non Fiction and Westerns

Special interest titles available in large print are:
The Little Oxford Dictionary
Music Book, Song Book
Hymn Book, Service Book

Also available from us courtesy of Oxford University Press:
Young Readers' Dictionary
(large print edition)
Young Readers' Thesaurus
(large print edition)

For further information or a free brochure, please contact us at:
Ulverscroft Large Print Books Ltd.,
The Green, Bradgate Road, Anstey,
Leicester, LE7 7FU, England.
Tel: (00 44) **0116 236 4325**
Fax: (00 44) **0116 234 0205**

Other titles in the
Linford Romance Library:

NIGHT MUSIC

Margaret Mounsdon

Marian and Georges, world-famous stars of classical music, are very much in love — though neither knows much about the other's past. One freezing night, while sheltering with Georges from a blizzard in an old barn, Marian's deepest secret comes back to haunt her in the most unexpected way, and she soon finds herself in danger from a stalker and a psychopath as she struggles to put together the missing pieces of her life. Will Georges still love her in the end — if they both make it through alive?

THE APOTHECARY'S DAUGHTER

June Davies

Keziah Sephton is kept busy caring for three generations of her family, as well as running the family apothecary shop. George Cunliffe has loved Keziah since they were youngsters, and when Benedict Clay arrives at the shop claiming to be blood kin, and is welcomed into the heart of the family, George is immediately suspicious of the soft-spoken Southern gentleman's motives ... After her grandmother's precious Book of Hours disappears, Keziah is tormented by treacherous doubts and swiftly enmeshed in a shocking spiral of deception, betrayal, ruthless ambition — and cold-blooded murder.